Dr. Kildare's™ Search

Max Brand™

G.K. Hall & Co.
Thorndike, Maine

Published in Large Print by arrangement with The Golden
West Literary Agency in conjunction with Laurence
Pollinger, Ltd.

G.K. Hall Large Print Book Series.

Printed on acid free paper in Great Britain.

Set in 16 Pt. Plantin.

Library of Congress Cataloging-in-Publication Data

Brand, Max, 1892–1944.
  Dr. Kildare's search / by Max Brand.
    p.   cm.
  ISBN 0-8161-5896-7 (alk. paper : lg. print)
  1. Kildare, Doctor (Fictitious character)—Fiction.
2. Physicians—United States—Fiction.   3. Large type
books.   I. Title.   II. Title: Dr. Kildare's hardest case.
  [PS3511.A87D73   1994]   93–34676
  813'.52—dc20   CIP

DR. KILDARE'S SEARCH

CHAPTER ONE

In the crowded waiting room of Dr. Gillespie there were people of ten nations of more than ten degrees, from the old pugilist with rheumatism in his broken hands to the Indian mystic whose eyes already were forgetting this world; but little Florie Adams took precedence over all of these. Her mother lagged breathless, a step behind, as Florie was led quickly on by a nurse so pretty that the little girl had to keep looking up at that freshness and that bloom; and so her stumbling feet forgot their way.

'Emergency!' said the nurse to the Negro who was on duty as though to guard the door. 'Emergency, Conover!'

So they came to the threshold and the mother leaned over the child, saying: 'He's a great man, Florie. He's a great, *great* man; and you just look at him and listen at him, and he'll make you well!'

Then the door opened and little Florie entered, prepared to listen with all her soul, and to see. She saw an office worn and old and littered, with the smell of a drugstore and the look of a secondhand furniture shop. She saw a young man in white with a pale face and eyes darkly stained by sleeplessness; he seemed to Florie like someone who has

1

stared too long and too hard at intangible, fading things; there was about him the humility and the tension of a foreigner who listens to speech that is only partially understood. But the great man was not he. The great man sat yonder in a wheelchair. To Florie he was as old as her private conception of the deity, and like her God he wore a tangled radiance of white hair, thin and luminous. He had a high forehead with a blue vein of wrath etched across it; he had the smile of a fighting Irishman who may be delighting in the battle or suffering from a twist of exquisite pain; and beyond all else he had eyes of fire that made Florie forget the rest. He barked at the pretty nurse in a harsh voice: 'Well, Lamont, what's this?'

'An emergency, Dr. Gillespie,' she answered.

Florie expected her to shrink, but there seemed no fear in her; she even smiled at this great and terrible doctor.

'It's scarlet fever, Dr. Gillespie,' said the mother. 'Little Joanie, she come down exactly like this; but I thought maybe there's a way of...'

'Never mind what you thought,' snarled the great Gillespie. 'What the devil is this, anyway?'

The last words were for another nurse who had come in with a tray that she placed across the arms of the wheelchair.

2

'It's two boiled eggs with some toast and crisp bacon crumbled into them,' said the nurse.

'Take the stuff away!' shouted Gillespie. 'Take it away and bring me coffee!'

The young doctor, in the meantime, sat on his heels and took the hand of Florie with a touch so gentle, so firm, so assured, that she could not help feeling that everything would be all right, if only the terrible old man would stop roaring. She smiled at him and he smiled back as he scanned her face deliberately, reading it up, reading it down.

'I'm sorry, sir,' the nurse of the tray was saying. 'It was orders to bring this.'

'By the jumping thunder—by the living ... whose orders?' boomed Gillespie.

'Dr. Kildare, sir.'

'Kildare!' exploded the great voice.

'Yes, sir?' answered the young man who sat on his heels.

Florie trembled, but this Kildare did not even turn his head from the examination as he spoke.

'And what am I to say is the meaning of this?' said the terrible voice. 'About this confounded interference, what am I to do?'

'If I were you, I would eat the eggs, sir. You've had nothing since yesterday.'

He rose as he spoke and kept on smiling down at Florie. The wrath of the great Gillespie dissolved.

'Not since yesterday? Haven't I, Jimmy?' he said, apologetically. But instantly he was barking: 'Where's the coffee, Parker?'

His anger drove her back toward the wall.

'It wasn't ordered for the tray, Dr. Gillespie,' she said.

'I'm to be treated like a babe in swaddling clothes, am I?' demanded Gillespie. 'You think I'm going to put up with this damned outrage? Well, get out of my sight! What are you waiting for, Nosy?'

The nurse vanished.

'Bring the child to me,' commanded Gillespie.

'Certainly, sir, when you've finished eating,' said Kildare.

And still the lightning did not fall!

'It's a simple case,' went on Kildare. And he said with that wonderfully gentle and quiet voice that opened the heart of Florie: 'She's been having aspirin, hasn't she?'

'Oh, yes,' said the mother.

'I wouldn't give her any more just now,' suggested young Dr. Kildare. 'Aspirin is a very good thing, but sometimes it will bring out a bit of a rash, like this.'

'Is that all it is?' gasped Mrs. Adams. 'Oh, Dr. Gillespie, is this right?'

'Right?' boomed Gillespie. 'Why, the young fool doesn't dare to be wrong, does he?'

So Florie was drawn out of the room, still

4

with her head turned to catch her last close view of greatness.

'Why did Mary Lamont bring that case in here?' Gillespie growled. 'It could have gone through other avenues...'

'Perhaps Mrs. Adams is a sister of Mike Ryan, sir,' suggested Kildare.

'Mike Ryan? The ignorant bartender in the saloon over there?'

'Yes, sir; my old friend Mike Ryan.'

'Next patient!' called Gillespie. 'You've got a taste for low company,' he added with his growl, 'that may drag you down to the gutter. And don't say: "Yes, sir," to that!'

'No, sir,' said Kildare.

There was a commotion in the outer office, a hurrying of heavy feet, a confusion of voices.

The door was broken open and a burly ambulance driver with a prize fighter's jaw and the bright little eyes of a pig came in, supporting a man doubled-up with pain. At the door appeared Conover, complaining: 'I tried to keep them out, Dr. Gillespie!'

'Never mind him, Joe,' said the big man. 'Here's the little old doc, and he'll fix you up. He fixes everybody up. He can look right through you like an X-ray.'

Joe, slumped in a chair, managed to whisper, with a twisting grin: 'Then he'll see the slug that McCarthy left inside of me five years ago.'

'What d'you mean by this, Weyman?' demanded Gillespie. 'Do you think this is the regular emergency ward, or what?'

Weyman, his cap in his hand, began backing up with small steps, only taking note that Kildare, on his knees, already was at work on the patient.

'Yeah, sure—emergency room,' said Weyman, 'only it was farther away—and I thought about how fast the Doc is, here—and Joe is a pal of mine...'

'Get out!' commanded Gillespie, and Weyman disappeared, saying hastily as he went through the door: 'Doc, he's even got the same name as me! We was raised on the same block!'

'By the same cops with the same nightsticks,' commented Gillespie, suddenly grinning. 'Let me get at that boy, Jimmy!'

'It's all right, sir, I've got it ... Stomach pains for several years, Joe?'

'Yeah, Doc. Off'n on. But this one—it's different—it's a sock in the eye...'

Pain cut off his breath. The smile he was trying to give turned into a ghastly, white contortion.

'How long has this pain been going on? ... Nurse, ring Killefer in surgery. I've got a job for him. A rush job ... And get an orderly here to take him ... How long has this been going on, Joe?'

'Since about five this morning ... I

thought it'd pass...'

'And the pain went down lower?'

'Yes. And then I remembered about you—because I was scared.'

'Ten hours?' murmured Kildare. 'I wish you'd remembered me sooner...'

As the orderly appeared with the wheeled stretcher, Kildare picked up Joe and laid him on his side on the table.

He said, briefly: 'Dr. Killefer—ruptured gastric ulcer—ten hours old. Tell Killefer.'

Kildare gripped Joe's hand and followed the stretcher to the door.

'I'll see you through, Joe,' he said.

'Will you? That's swell!' murmured Joe, and relaxed, his eyes closing over their story of pain.

'More of your low company, Kildare,' said Gillespie. 'I see you're the "doc" to the whole district, now. When any ragamuffin pickpocket, yegg, or second-story man speaks of "the doc," he means young Dr. Kildare. And what do *you* get out of it? For the sake of a fugitive rat with a bullethole in him, you slap down the authorities, kick the hospital in the face, and damn near ruin yourself; and what would they do for you?'

'I don't know,' said Kildare, thoughtfully, 'but I think some of them would die for us—and they're the only ones who would.'

CHAPTER TWO

The call of 'Next Patient!' brought in a sallow-faced youth of twenty-two and his personal physician, a Dr. Arthur Sloan, who kept the sprightly verve of an athlete at fifty-five. 'You have the case history and the laboratory reports already, Dr. Gillespie,' said Sloan.

'Good,' said Gillespie, 'and now I have the man! Arthur Sloan is a known and experienced physician, Kildare, but you may be able to help him.'

'I'll try, sir,' said Kildare.

Dr. Sloan stiffened.

'I hoped for your personal attention to a very baffling case, Dr. Gillespie,' he said.

'You'll have it if it's needed,' said Gillespie. 'But Kildare does something more than fill time-gaps around here. He won't waste many minutes if he hasn't an idea.'

'Very well,' said Sloan, coldly, 'if you'll remove the bathrobe, Mr. Loring...'

Kildare went briskly ahead with his examination.

'This case has been worked up thoroughly,' said Dr. Sloan, who from the corner of his eye seemed to condemn every gesture Kildare was making. 'It seems a characteristic case of chronic malaria ... you

8

know that we come from a malarial district. Mr. Loring is losing strength and appetite, together with weight. He has a degree or two of fever in the afternoons. Classical symptoms, you'll agree. But I bring him here because I've been unable to find the malarial plasmodia in any of the blood smears. However, it *must* be malaria!'

'I'm afraid that I can't agree with you, Dr. Sloan,' said Kildare, stepping back a little.

'Ah, *you* don't agree?' asked Sloan, smiling a little. 'After your *very* brief examination, what do *you* think it may be?'

'Bacterio endocarditis,' said Kildare.

'My dear young man!' said Sloan, and shrugged his shoulders in resignation.

'What's that?' asked Gillespie. 'Bacterio endocarditis? You're not trying to be original?'

'No, sir.'

'*Quite* a bit out of the way, I should say,' commented Sloan.

'You've taken the blood smears at different times of the day, Sloan?' asked Gillespie.

'Yes, sir. Repeated smears, and always at varying hours.'

'Is that what you base it on?' Gillespie demanded of Kildare. 'Because the plasmodia have not been found you're sure that it couldn't be chronic malaria?'

'No, sir,' Kildare answered, 'because I

9

know that frequently the malarial organisms may be located in the spleen and remain there, acting as a reservoir for infection.'

'The spleen palpable?' demanded Gillespie.

'Quite,' said Sloan.

'For a first guess—I haven't had my hands on Loring yet—but for a first guess, I can't help feeling that you're right, Sloan. Kildare, you're barking up the wrong tree.'

'I believe not, sir.'

'Damn the beliefs—I want the proofs. You're not guessing, are you?'

'No, sir, not entirely.'

'You've been too quick, Kildare,' said Gillespie, shaking his head. 'What about the heart?'

'There's a systolic murmur of the apex, transmitted to the axilla,' reported Kildare.

'That is true,' agreed Sloan, grudgingly.

'But at the same time, that doesn't make it bacterio endocarditis, Kildare!' exclaimed Gillespie.

'If young Dr. Kildare were to come down into our country,' said Sloan, with a sour smile, 'he would learn a little more about some of the curious phases of malaria. It's not always something that a bit of quinine will rub out.'

Kildare set his teeth hard and endured. He was sweating and his anger kept his eyes fixed straight ahead, but his voice remained under control.

'Young men,' growled Gillespie, 'should learn not to jump their opinions into the dark. Kildare, I'd be glad to hear you admit that you're wrong about this.'

'I can't do that, sir,' said Kildare.

Gillespie stared suddenly at his assistant. 'Kildare, what have you seen?'

'Mr. Loring,' said Kildare, disregarding Gillespie's question, 'are there fleas in your part of the country?'

'For God's sake,' cried Loring, 'what has that to do with anything?'

Kildare pointed to four or five small spots at the base of Loring's throat.

'A slight rash or irritation of some sort,' said Sloan, indifferently.

'*Are* there fleas in your country?' insisted Kildare.

'Not many. Not in *my* house,' declared Loring.

'Petechiae, then,' said Kildare, and stepped back to indicate that he had finished speaking his mind.

'I suppose we can go on, then, with the question of the chronic malaria?' asked Sloan.

'Chronic malaria?' said Gillespie, wheeling his chair closer and staring at the little spots on the throat. 'Certainly not. They *are* petechiae—and absolutely diagnostic. It's bacterio endocarditis, man, and the search is finished.'

'You mean that *he* is right?' demanded Loring.

'Unfortunately, yes,' said Gillespie.

'Extraordinary!' growled Sloan. 'Absolutely extraordinary!'

Kildare, when they had left the room, ran a handkerchief over his sweating face.

'I was hard on you, eh?' demanded Gillespie.

'Not particularly, sir.'

'Yes, I was hard on you, and in front of strangers. I hoped that you'd seen something but I couldn't be sure. And so I made you sweat. Because if you *had* been taking a shot in the dark, I would have wanted to crucify you in front of the whole world. It's a damnable temptation for doctors to make a brilliant guess—and then stick to it like stubborn mules. Understand that?'

'Yes, sir.'

'But there's another thing that's more important still: When you think you're right, when you're honestly convinced, then it's your opinion against the whole world. That's the time to nail your flag to the mast the way you did just now. You weren't entirely sure that those petechiae *were* absolutely diagnostic?'

'Not entirely, sir.'

'But it was your best thought on the subject, and so you stuck to it. Oh, Jimmy,

12

there are times when every doctor has to act quickly. There's life or death hanging on whether he thinks right, but there's no time to ask questions. Those are the moments when a doctor has a shudder up his spinal column and his knees are watery and his heart is sick, but all the while he has to talk and act like God Almighty. Will you remember that?'

'Yes, sir,' said Kildare. 'Shall I call the next patient?'

'Don't change the subject on me. Hide your own pride, if you want to, but don't try to cover up the fact that old Gillespie was wrong, just now. I've made mistakes before; I'll make 'em again; and old or young, all a doctor can do is his best.'

He leaned back in his chair with closed eyes.

'Let me get you something,' urged Kildare.

'For what? Can't an old man be tired and close his eyes? Get me something for what?'

'For the pain,' said Kildare.

'There's no pain!'

'Very well, sir. There's no pain, then.'

'How do you know there's pain?'

'You have two ways of smiling. One way is when it has you by the throat.'

'Tommyrot! Nothing has me by the throat.'

'The melanoma...'

'Be still about that.'

'Why can't we speak about it?'

'Because there's no cure for me, and what's the use of a dead man talking about death?'

'We can't cure you,' said Kildare, steadily, 'but we can stretch out your time. There's a fire burning you up, and you give it nothing but your body to feed on. I have to fight to make you eat one small meal a day. Carson could help you with his new treatment.'

'You mean his new system for "drinking" X-rays?'

'You won't see him. You won't lift a hand to help yourself.'

'I've had my three score and ten,' said Gillespie. 'Just why should I try to stay here—in a slow fire—dying inch by inch? Why should I try to steal time that doesn't belong to me?'

Kildare started to speak but the words would not pass his lips.

'Go on! Tell me!' roared Gillespie suddenly.

'You've got to stay on because of me,' said Kildare, at last.

'I do, do I?' cried Gillespie, apparently in a rage.

Kildare walked deliberately to the lion and laid a hand on his shoulder.

'I'd never be able to take half of what you know, half of what you can give the world,'

14

said Kildare, 'but you have to wait until you've loaded me with all I can stagger under.'

The old man, half-closing his eyes, drew a long, shuddering, groaning breath. He dropped his head on his breast and laid a hand on that of Kildare.

'Jimmy,' he said, and fighting hard he started again: 'Jimmy...'

'Next patient!' called Kildare.

'Ay,' muttered Gillespie. 'The next patient. You'll have your own damned way about everything, I suppose.'

'Next patient in one moment, sir,' said Conover, opening the door a trifle.

'You'll let me have Carson in?'

'I suppose so.'

'And you'll follow his regime?'

'Jimmy,' said Gillespie, making a gesture with both hands, 'what right have I to deny that so long as I live I have hope? I preach miracles every day; why shouldn't I pretend that one might be worked on me? Go as far as you like. Does that make you happy?'

CHAPTER THREE

When the sun came out, the mild weather had to be used. From two angles of the second story windows of the Blair General

15

Hospital there is a good view of the tennis courts where the internes and doctors get a bit of exercise now and then. A good many of those windows were filled, this afternoon, for there was something worth watching on the courts where Dr. Hendrix, who had been a national figure in tennis ten years before, had met his match. A tall, blond young athlete, not half so racket-wise as Hendrix, was covering the court like a tiger.

Mary Lamont was leaning over one of those window sills when Kildare stopped behind her.

'You like him pretty well,' said Kildare.

She looked back over her shoulder, saying: 'How do you know?'

'That's easy. You never turn your head. You're looking at a man, not a tennis game.'

'You ought to be a detective; they *pay* for eyes, in that business.'

'It's Gregory Lane,' he announced.

'Oh, you know him? What do *you* think he's like?'

'He's just a shade under six feet; weighs a hundred and eighty; has stiff hair and uses a little slick 'em on it; a good forehead and a pair of gray-green eyes; speaks a shade from the right side of his mouth but laughs all over; stands straight, has a light step and a heavy pair of shoulders.'

'A regular police description!'

'Want to know some more about him?'

16

'Yes. Go ahead as far as you can.'

'He's been well-raised; had some of his education in England; likes the Hemingway sort of writing; has a fighting disposition; is nervous before the fight begins; loves a good joke; and sleeps on his face.'

'Jimmy! You've never even shaken hands with him?'

'What of it?'

'Then how could you know he was well-raised?'

'Well, manners are made at home. He's been handled with care. The England appears a bit in his accent; but sometimes he talks a trifle Hemingway; he looks ready to punch any man in the chin but he's easily startled—so is a wild cat; he has a lot of smiling wrinkles in his face even at twenty-nine; and as for sleeping on his face, I've seen him very early in the morning.'

'You're just an X-ray, Jimmy,' she said, rather petulantly.

'I've never been able to see through you,' he answered.

'But he's not nervous, really,' she said.

'No? Look down there now. He's going to lose that point.'

Dr. Gregory Lane and Dr. Hendrix were in the midst of a base-line rally, the ball sweeping back and forth low over the net.

'He *won't* lose it!' declared Mary Lamont.

'He will, though,' said Kildare. 'You see,

17

he's trying to make himself go to the net, but he's a little afraid ... There he goes!'

Gregory Lane, caught completely out of position, flubbed a half volley into the net.

'You had no right to know that he'd do that!' protested Mary Lamont, turning on Kildare.

'But he's a good fellow; he's a good sport,' said Kildare. 'See him laugh—and it's a set point, too.'

'He *is* a good fellow,' argued Mary Lamont, half to herself. 'And besides, he'll never be caught that way again.'

'Won't he? I tell you, Hendrix, the old fox, has his number, now. He'll keep trapping him to the end of time ... look at that!'

Lane was serving, and again Hendrix worked the forehand slice short; again a half volley was dubbed, this time out of court.

'I don't want to watch any more,' said the girl. 'Not with you standing around. I don't want you to see Gregory Lane being beaten.'

'But he'll do better, now.'

'He won't! Look at the way he overdrove that one!'

'That's all right. He'll keep on overdriving them until he gets the feel of the ball again ... Oh, there's a lot more to him than I thought!'

Lane began to whip the ball long and hard into the base-line corners and Hendrix, with years telling a bit upon him, lost some of his control.

'He'll begin to get the net now. He's feeling his oats. I told you that he was a fighter, but he's nervous until he sees the first blood—his own or the other fellow's.'

As though inspired by this remark, Lane sprinted to the net and cut a return into an impossible place for Hendrix.

'Don't look at it any more,' said the girl.

'Why not, Mary?'

'Because you know too much. There's only one thing you don't know.'

'Thousands of things, of course.'

'About Gregory Lane, I mean. You can't guess what makes him so extra attractive to the girls.'

'Of course, I can. He's a magnificent looking fellow.'

'It isn't what you see, though.'

'What is it, then?'

'A private income.'

'Ah, is that it?'

'Jimmy, will you please be a little bit jealous?'

'Partly jealous, but chiefly helpless and hopeless, you know.'

'I don't want you to be that way, either.'

'All right, you tell me what to be.'

'I don't know,' she said, shaking her head. 'But I hate the whole world—that's all I know.'

'Suppose I had as much as—well, what

would it have to be.'

'I've got all the minimums worked out, rent, laundry, food—are you always hungry, Jimmy?'

'Yes. Always.'

She sighed.

'I could fill you up with porridge and things. They cost a lot of gas to cook, but they're the cheapest. Could you eat them?'

'I could eat anything.'

'And then there's light and gas, and installment payments on the furniture...'

'Suppose we rented a furnished place?'

'Jimmy, you simply don't know anything. Furnished places are just ruin!'

'Are they?'

'Of course, they are! ... And then there's clothing, and that's a dreadful item. And then we'd leave out everything like gifts, and amusements, and incidentals—except that you're so *horribly* absent-minded, Jimmy.'

'I wouldn't be, though. I'd tie strings around my fingers in the morning and hitch labels to them.'

'Cutting everything to the minimum, Jimmy, we'd have to have one hundred dollars a week—if we wanted to be decent and not just rats in a hole.'

'One hundred—dollars—a week!' murmured Kildare. 'And just now I'm getting one hundred a month...'

She put out her hands to him.

20

'Haven't I reason to hate the world?' she asked.

CHAPTER FOUR

Winter, which had retreated the day before, seemed to have disappeared the next morning and a misplaced day of spring warmed up the dark streets of New York and set people smiling unaware. Gillespie himself, as he answered the telephone, was looking out the window at that blue, summer sky.

'Yes, Carew,' he said, to the head of the hospital, 'yes, but why does Gray want Kildare? ... He can't have him for that! ... Kildare *is* carrying on as a regular interne, but he's done enough appendectomies ... Besides, we're busy, today ... we're taking a day off in the country!'

He slammed up the telephone and said: 'Did you hear that, Jimmy? We're going for a ride in the country. The next thing is to find a car to take us, free, and a place to go ... Call that rich pal of yours ... Get Messenger on the phone for me.'

He was saying a moment later: 'Messenger, you've been asking me to come out with Kildare and see that medical plant you're starting. What about today? ... Good, then ... We *could* use a car, at that. Will you be out there? I'll look at your plant as far as a wheelchair can take me, and Kildare will go the rest of the way.'

Mary Lamont came in, dressed for the street in a small black hat and a green coat that looked too slim and trim for winter weather.

'The report you wanted on the Clonmel case, Doctor,' she said, giving Kildare a long envelope, and she started in haste from the office.

'Lamont!' called Gillespie. 'What are you doing out of white?'

'It's my day off, Doctor,' she said.

'Wait a minute,' he commanded. 'You believe in telepathy, Jimmy?'

'Half and half,' said Kildare.

'We got it from Lamont, this idea of a day off,' insisted Gillespie. 'Lamont, got a date?'

'Yes, Doctor.'

'Of course, you have. It's with us. We're going for a cruise into the country. Jimmy, get into your street clothes ... Get Nosy Parker to lay out my own things and lend me a hand.'

The winter cold and wet had glazed the trees, the shrubs. The whole countryside flamed around them off to the verge of the horizon blue, which seemed to dwell in a permanent twilight.

'There's something wrong with Lamont,'

22

said Gillespie, a bit later. 'Find out what it is, Jimmy.'

'What is it, Lamont?' he asked, smiling a little.

'It's a job for Dr. Gillespie,' she said.

'Won't Kildare do?' asked Gillespie.

'Not a bit. There's a great surgeon in the Blair General that's going to be hounded out of his place by bad luck and unpleasant people in the front office.'

'What great surgeon? And how great is he?'

'He has a beautiful pair of hands,' she said, 'and—he's wonderfully fast! Yet the hospital is going to do him in because he's had bad luck. Unless you'll say the good word for him, Dr. Gillespie.'

'Young and beautiful, ain't he?' asked Gillespie.

'Yes.'

'So, of *course*, he's a great surgeon.'

'He's Gregory Lane,' she said, defiantly.

'The new man on the staff? What about him, Kildare?'

'I've heard good things, sir. I don't know him very well.'

'He's lost his last six cases in a row,' said Mary Lamont, 'but every one of them was a frightful mess. He's a neuro-surgeon, you know. Dr. Gillespie, will you help him?'

'If he's worth help, I may. Six in a row? Well, that may happen to the best—in brain surgery.'

'*Will* you help him?'

'What's he mean to you?'

'I love him,' she said.

'Bah!' said Gillespie.

'I do,' she declared. 'He's wonderful—and so quiet—and he's so much of a man! I *love* him!'

'All right,' said Gillespie. 'If she loves him right out loud like this, in public, there's nothing for you to worry about, Jimmy.'

'You don't know Mary,' said Kildare. 'She can be bitter.'

'You *will* help him?' insisted the girl, overlooking Kildare.

'I'll try.'

'Thank you, Doctor,' she said, setting back with a sigh of relief.

Five minutes later they had turned off the road down a driveway bordered by lofty poplars and so they came to what seemed not a rigid institution with prison-like structures, but an open-faced New England village.

'Is this the place?' said Gillespie. 'See what Messenger has done! He's turned a village into a medical apparatus. A man like Messenger is so rich that he can afford to use his brains, eh? Oh, lucky devil! Where's Messenger waiting for us?'

'He's in the cottage of the assistant professor of Humane Research, sir,' said the driver.

'Humane Research!' said Gillespie. 'Now, what the devil might that be? *All* of medicine is humane research, I hope.'

When they drew up at the appointed place and had helped Gillespie back into his wheelchair, Messenger's daughter came down the steps, waving, and calling out; and big Messenger himself hurried after her. He helped get the wheelchair up the steps and into the house. They went back into a library where a fire burned on a five foot hearth and a Persian rug glowed like a field in May with green and red and gold.

'The chair of Humane Research,' said Messenger, explaining to Gillespie, 'is a title, as you can imagine, that covers a great many things because it's the general name of the whole institution; and I'm advised that if I get the right man for it, he could have an interesting life. You see—the holder of this chair is to have carte blanche. I hope to get a man who has a peculiar insight into diseases that may be a little more in the imagination than in fact—a man with a gift for stepping into the full confidence of people, you know.'

'Ah?' said Gillespie. 'That's an unusual idea. And I like it. Have anybody in mind?'

'Someone I wanted to talk over with you. I have some of the other chairs well filled; for instance, there'll be Tillinghast of Chicago in neurology...'

'A *great* man,' said Gillespie. 'A very great man.'

'There will be an orthopedist. Grover Jackson has consented to come for that chair.'

'You couldn't do better than Jackson,' said Gillespie. 'The idiot is only right part of the time; but even his mistakes are inspired ones.'

'The pediatrician is to be Professor Johann Herz.'

'Great Scott, how did you manage to land him?'

'I kept bidding and waiting, and bidding again.'

'I'm glad I didn't see this before,' sighed Gillespie. 'I would have been tempted to try to find a place for myself. But who have you in mind for this chair of Humane Research, this cream of the whole lot?'

'A younger man, Dr. Gillespie.'

Messenger paused a moment. Then he said: 'It seemed to Nancy and me—she's done more about this scheme than I have—that there couldn't be a better man than the fellow who first interested us in medicine—I mean to say, we felt that if we could give a new, free life to the man who gave back life and more than life to Nancy—in a word, our choice is Dr. Kildare, if you approve.'

Suddenly he was smiling, and standing back a little with a genial expectancy. Nancy looked happily toward Kildare. She saw him go straight to Gillespie, staring sharply down into his face. After that, he turned and glanced toward Mary Lamont; and what Nancy saw in the face of the nurse was as old as hunger, and as bright as the sun.

Old Gillespie took off his glasses and squinted his eyes at the thought that had been presented to him. He polished the glasses and put them on again. At last he seemed able to see something.

'The trouble with filling a post like this,' said Gillespie, 'is that you'd need a man who would never be satisfied with what he had done but would have a spur in his ribs urging him forward. You'd want a man whom other people could trust. He'd have to be a man without fear of opinions but loyal to his friends, while he was loyal to the truth. He'd have to be capable of growth so that in the end he'd be worthy of heading what may be one of the most important medical centers in the world.

'He'd have to be a man who had been tested to the heart and to the marrow of the bone. That's why I can freely say that if you searched the world over, I don't think you could make a better choice than Dr. Kildare!'

He dropped his head and stared at the

27

floor, as though seriously questioning his decision before he reaffirmed it.

'You couldn't find a better choice than that,' he concluded.

Messenger said: 'I hoped that you'd say that, Dr. Gillespie, but I wasn't entirely sure. I knew that you had your own great plans for Jimmy.'

'My own plans for him? What plans could I have that would be half so good as this chance to give his gifts to the world and to have the money curse removed from him before it has a chance to break his heart—or his back?'

CHAPTER FIVE

The great Gillespie did not often allow his imagination free scope, but on the return trip he seemed in the highest spirits and sketched for Kildare a future as bright and rich as a golden crown. Mary Lamont watched him with a growing content that reached a happy climax when he said: 'How could you have told them that you wanted a day to think it over? How could you keep from accepting on the spot?'

'I remembered what a fairly intelligent fellow said to me, once,' answered Kildare.

'What was it?'

'He said that the obvious choice was usually the quick regret.'

'Sounds like some damned coiner of aphorisms. There's nothing I hate more,' said Gillespie, 'than young or old fools who try to say things so neatly that they'll be easily remembered. Who was this precious dunderhead?'

'His name is Leonard Gillespie,' said Kildare.

*   *   *

At seven that evening Kildare called Mary Lamont. 'Have you a date this evening?' he asked.

'Yes. Is it something important?'

'Well, to me it is.'

'All right. I'll call off the date.'

'Will you? Then meet me over at Mike's in a few minutes?'

'I'd rather not Mike's, Jimmy.'

'But I only have half an hour. Then I'm back on duty.'

'I'll be at Mike's,' she said, and dropped the receiver heavily into the cradle.

When she got over, she found him in the family room with a glass of beer.

'We oughtn't to meet here,' she said. 'People will see us; and the internes are not supposed to go out with nurses.'

'Nobody who sees us in here will talk,' he

answered.

'Anyway, perhaps it doesn't matter?' she suggested.

He seemed to hear her dimly; a mist of thought clouded his eyes.

'You look a bit dressed up,' he said. 'What have you got under that cloak?'

'It's a lace thing.'

'Let me see it.'

She opened the cloak.

'Leave the cloak off for a while, will you?'

'This isn't the dress for a place like this.'

'It's the dress for me. All right. Put the cloak back on. Did you have to break the date?'

'I stalled it a little. He'll wait.'

'Who's the he?'

'It's none of your business.'

'Who's the he?'

'Gregory Lane.'

'Who's Gregory Lane?'

'Jimmy, what's the matter with you?'

'Nothing; I'm all right.'

'Oh, but there *is* something wrong. You have that look as though you'd been driving fast all day—and were going to drive all night. What is it you're going to do?'

'Nothing.'

'Jimmy, that isn't true. Look! I thought today that I was going to be the happiest girl in the world; now you're about to tell me that it's all no good.'

He said nothing. He took a drink of beer and seemed to find it bitter.

'Jimmy!'

'Yes?'

'You're not taking the Messenger offer! You're staying here! You're staying with Gillespie!'

'Mary, you like Gregory Lane a lot, don't you?'

'Will you answer me?'

'You like Lane a lot, don't you?'

She had been rising from her chair. Now she sank back into it slowly, staring at him.

'Yes, I like him a lot. More than almost anyone I know.'

'How much does he like you?'

'Quite a lot, it seems.'

'Does he want to marry you?'

'Yes.'

'But you let him wait and came over here to me in Mike's saloon?'

She kept staring at him, frightened.

'That doesn't matter,' she said.

'Giving up the Messenger job doesn't count,' he said. 'It's giving up you that hurts.'

'You *have* given it up!' whispered Mary. She put her face in her hands.

'I'd gone as far,' she said, 'as the color of the nursery walls.' Then, looking up, she said, in an agony: 'Oh, Jimmy, why, why have you done it?'

'It's no sacrifice,' he told her. 'Gillespie is worth everything.'

'Honor,' she said bitterly, 'and the Right, and all the rest of the capitals. I guessed it! But I wouldn't believe that you'd be such a—No, I don't mean that.'

She took hard hold on herself. His words were calm but his face was gray with suffering.

'It wasn't a question of right or wrong,' he persisted. 'There were two bids. That was all. And I sold out to the higher one. Messenger means an easy life for me, and all that. A home—and all that. It even means having you. Gillespie means a hard grind but he's stored up a thousand years of things I must know. It's no sacrifice.'

'A home, and children, and I—we don't count compared with Gillespie?' she said.

Kildare could not answer.

After a while she was able to master herself. 'I guess there isn't much left to us,' she said.

'No,' he answered. 'Only what you say is left.'

'I make the rules and we still play a game?'

'Can we?'

'Yes. But we're back at something we've known about before—one hundred dollars a month.'

'I know,' said Kildare.

'No. You don't know. You've never

32

wanted what a woman wants, so you don't know. Oh, I could say a lot of things!'

'Go ahead. I'll listen.'

'I know you will. There's nothing wrong with you, except the bulldog. The big things you go after, you lock your jaws on and won't let go. There's nothing wrong with me, either, except wanting what a woman has a right to. It's queer, isn't it? To be heartsick, I mean, and yet with nothing to feel guilty about.'

'Queer? Yes, it's that. You're going to be late for Gregory Lane.'

'Stop it, Jimmy. You care more than that, don't you?'

'Yes.'

'You're going to have empty, lonely times; and when they come, you call for me. Will you?'

'Will it be all right?'

'We'll make it all right. If there's something—something—more important—then I won't come.'

They looked at one another.

'You're right. Everything you say is right. Go on,' said Kildare.

'But if there's nothing more important—then I'll come to you whenever you want, and wherever. I've got some money; you've got some too: not much, but we'll go as far as it will take us ... around the corner ... up the street ... and back again...'

'It'll be the wasting of you, Mary.'

'No. It's good for a woman to be used. As far as God will let her. We'll go as far as we can—without talking of certain things. We'll go as far as we can and try to forget that we're just walking about on the outside of things. It'll be just pretending.'

'It won't be pretending. Not for me,' said Kildare.

'But oh, Jimmy, if you won't be sick of it with all the hope left out, I'll be everything to you that I can be; all the things that begin with good morning and finish with good night.'

CHAPTER SIX

It was next morning before Gillespie had word. He had his black man, Conover, heaping up stuff in the inner office, which served as a semi-laboratory as well; and the piled notebooks of Kildare, the records of experiments and cases, were being packed by Conover with more dispatch than neatness, for Gillespie hurried him on.

'Let's be done with it, Conover,' said Gillespie. 'Don't hang and dawdle like that, man!'

'But look at the words that fill up the books!' said Conover. 'Think of him drawing them out, late at night. Think of him remembering what you've said and done all of every day and crowding it down like this! There ain't even a crap game that could keep me awake so long; not even if I was carryin' loaded dice, sir!'

'You confounded black idiot,' said Gillespie, 'I know you and your crooked dice too well. Get that stuff out of here and we'll be ready to go back to the old days, and a clean deck, and no damned foreign interference.'

The voice of Kildare said behind him: 'I hope not, sir. I've just telephoned to Mr. Messenger to thank him for his offer and to tell him that I'm staying on under you.'

The head of Gillespie jerked back.

'Ten thousand a year—a house—a gentleman's establishment—a chance for an honorable career—you're throwing that away for the sake of—and tell me another thing—come around here and face me!'

Instead, Kildare rested a hand on the back of the chair. Gillespie took one hasty glance over his shoulder and then quickly looked front again.

His voice had changed from a bullying uproar to gentleness: 'Did you tell this to Mary Lamont?'

'Yes, sir.'

'How long do you think that a girl will wait around? Do you think she's a Biblical character? Will she be patient for seven years?' demanded Gillespie, roaring suddenly again.

'No, sir,' said Kildare.

Gillespie winced as though a pain had touched him inwardly. After a moment, his fingers began to tap softly on the arm of the wheelchair.

'Give me the telephone,' he said. 'We're wasting time. There's a day's work ahead of us.'

Kildare silently passed him the telephone.

'Get me Carew!' commanded Gillespie of the operator. 'That you, Carew? I have to congratulate you. I hear you've got a pair of hands at last in neurosurgery that's able to do real work on the brain ... Young fellow—Gregory Lane ... I don't care what you think; the fellow's probably a genius. I want Kildare assigned to him to assist, when he's operating. Only then, mind you. Operations over, Kildare comes back to my office ... He'd be wasting an opportunity if he didn't do some work under Lane and I don't care what Lane's record is. Napoleon had a bad record too, at Leipzig and Waterloo. Good-by!'

That was how Kildare found himself, late that afternoon, working beside Gregory Lane in the surgery and admiring what seemed to him a matchless technique. The brain surgeon handles at one moment hard bone;

36

the next he is tying off thin blood vessels and dealing with the most delicate tissue in the world. He works in a region where the least hemorrhage or pressure or lesion may cause death or a ruined brain that is worse than death. He needs a touch as sure as steel and as light as a feather. It seemed to Kildare that Lane had all of these qualities. He was young, but he was a master. It was one of those perfect operations; and just as it neared completion the patient died.

When they were taking off the masks and white gowns big Gregory Lane said: 'I know you want to be an internist, but you have a touch for this sort of work, also. That was a good job you did.'

Kildare thanked him and looked over the big man carefully. It would have been hard to find fault with this fellow, except for an apparent excess of pride. But he needed that pride now.

'I suppose Carew will ask you why I butcher so many in the surgery?' asked Gregory Lane. 'There's another—seven in a row!'

The naming of the disaster seemed to take all the heart out of him; his smile wavered and failed.

'I'm not here to spy. Gillespie sent me,' answered Kildare.

'Gillespie? Ah, that's different!'

'He'd heard that you were having bad luck

but that you were a good workman. If he asks what I think I can tell him that nothing about your work is wrong except the luck.' Sometimes there was a quick flash of enthusiasm in Kildare. It burned in his eyes now for a moment as he added: 'I thought it was a beautiful job, Doctor.'

Lane flushed a little.

'I needed that,' he said. 'And when you talk, Kildare, there's a saying in this hospital that it's almost like Gillespie speaking. I need a drink, too. What about it?'

CHAPTER SEVEN

Spring, which had for two days pretended to be returning to New York, ended in a cold rain which a northeaster turned to glass on the streets. The wind still was whining around corners when Dr. Carew called Gillespie the next morning to say: 'Sometimes I feel more like a headsman than a doctor, Leonard. I have to be the executioner, you know, and I hate the job, but today I suppose my course is clear. The reason I called you is because we talked about the man yesterday. It's Gregory Lane; seventh fatality in seven operations. I can't have a man like that in the hospital!'

'If you can't have him, I suppose you'll fire

him,' said Gillespie.

'I only wanted to check with you, Leonard.'

'Check with Kildare. He saw Lane at work.'

'And liked it?'

'Better than any he'd ever seen.'

'*Kildare* said that?'

'He did.'

'But seven deaths in seven operations...'

'He had seven lost cases handed to him in a row. That's all.'

'Then you think that I ought to keep him on?'

'I can't do your thinking for you. *I'd* keep him. That's all I know.'

That was why Gregory Lane was still on the staff of the Blair General Hospital when, an hour later, there was a call from the accident ward for a neurosurgeon. Already they had tucked around the patient the red blanket which means 'Emergency,' for it was a bad head injury. Dr. Gregory Lane was assigned, and a moment later a call came through for Kildare.

'Are you still assigned to assist Dr. Lane? ... Report to him in the emergency ward at once!'

The emergency ward is the no-man's land across which the shock troops of a hospital move into action; but nothing in the room took the eye of Kildare except the tall figure of Dr. Gregory Lane bent over a patient in a corner bed. It was a man of thirty-five or forty, unconscious, pale, so that his face looked like one of those fine-line Holbein drawings that express the character but give little of the life.

'That's worth something,' said Kildare.

'And we're going to work on him,' answered Lane. 'But it looks tough. I've rushed through an X-ray plate.'

He passed it to Kildare and went on: 'He's had the usual treatment for a skull fracture. It's an extradural hemorrhage; we'll have to operate if we want to save his life. Do you think?'

'I think so,' agreed Kildare, his forefinger on a wrist to follow the slowing beat of the pulse. 'Who is he?'

'We haven't any history. Traffic accident knocked him over; nothing on him except his name. Henry Thornton. Does that mean anything to you?'

'Not a thing.'

The eyes of Henry Thornton opened wide. He threw up a hand before his face and winced.

When he lowered his arm he said: 'I thought it still was coming at me.' Then he started to sit up. Kildare pushed him back.

'You're doing all right, Mr. Thornton,' he said.

'You've had a bad knock,' explained Lane.

'It was going right past me but it skidded,' breathed Thornton. 'I tried to jump—but my feet went out from under me.'

He sat up in spite of the restraining hand of Kildare.

'How long ago was it?' he demanded. 'What day is this? *What DAY is this?*'

'It's Tuesday,' said Kildare.

Thornton closed his eyes and gasped.

'Good—good—' he breathed. 'Morning or afternoon?'

'It's morning. It's about ten-thirty.'

'That's all right, then,' said Thornton. 'But I thought for a moment—for a moment it seemed to me that I was stymied—on a treadmill, so that I'd never get there—and I'd miss Friday noon!'

Even in his relief his excitement kept him tense. He shook off the effects of the sedative in an instant.

Gregory Lane commanded: 'You'll have to lie down, Mr. Thornton.'

'Lie down? Good God, no!' exclaimed Thornton. 'That's the last thing that I can do!'

'You must,' said Kildare, and pressed him slowly, gently back into the bed.

The tension of Thornton increased to a violent shuddering.

'That won't do—quiet yourself, Thornton!' said Lane.

Kildare, still controlling the patient, found

himself looking into desperate eyes. He said, quietly: 'The fact is that you've a bad injury; and it's necessary for you to lie still.'

'Head injury? It can't be bad. There's hardly an ache—there's—'

'It's a fracture,' said Kildare. 'We must operate, Mr. Thornton.'

'Operate?' said Thornton. 'Did you say—fracture—and operation?'

'That's better. Relax,' urged Kildare. 'That's what we want. No tension. It's bad for you.'

'Operation—' repeated Thornton slowly, tasting the bad news by degrees, deeply. He kept looking straight up at the ceiling as he said: 'Tell me how bad it is, will you?'

'It might be dangerous without treatment at once.'

'Dangerous?'

'Yes.'

'You mean—death?'

Kildare glanced up at the neurosurgeon. 'Yes,' said Lane. 'Without an immediate operation it might mean death.'

'Could I live till Friday without the operation?'

'That's unlikely.'

'Is it impossible?'

'We can't actually say that you'd die before Friday. But if you have any regard for your life...'

'Why do you talk to me about life? I've

had five years of dying. I refuse the operation!'

He started to get up and there was a little high-pitched, gasping sound from a nurse.

'We can't control you, Thornton,' said Kildare, 'but let me suggest something. Whatever it is you have to do on Friday, couldn't I manage it for you?'

'*You* do it for me? *You* go in my place?' murmured Thornton, the idea still strange to him.

'Tell me what your work is—tell me what is to happen Friday. I'll be there!'

'You would, I think,' said Thornton, reading deeply the mind of Kildare. 'I think you'll go for me and you *can* do it!'

'Tell me what it is,' urged Kildare.

'You'll leave everything and go?'

'I'll leave everything.'

Thornton lay back with his eyes closed, smiling faintly. 'You ought to have been a priest, not a doctor,' he said. 'You put me half to sleep. You make the whole thing seem finished already—and five years of hell are out the window and forgotten. Have you a notebook?'

'It's ready here.'

Thornton began: 'You have to start for—'

His voice stopped. Calamity entered his eyes and he started up on one elbow with a desperate face and then the blow which had been coming struck him back on his pillow, senseless.

Kildare got a stethoscope instantly over the breast of Thornton. The heart was still working, but with a horrible pause and stagger in the pulsation.

Then the loud-speaker in the next room began to intone: 'Dr. Kildare wanted in Dr. Gillespie's office. Emergency! ... Dr. Kildare wanted...'

Gregory Lane looked wildly about him, from Thornton, to Kildare, and thence into unanswering space.

Kildare said, 'He's still got a bit of life in him.'

'But I can't work on him. I can't operate. He distinctly refused the operation,' protested Lane.

'Did he?' said Kildare. 'I don't remember hearing that.'

Lane started and looked at Kildare again.

'Oh, but *I* do,' said the nurse. 'Oh, I *distinctly* remember that he refused the operation!'

Kildare looked on her with a sour eye. She flushed but she lifted her head; it was plain that she was one of the good Christians who will see right triumph, even if it costs a thousand lives.

In the next room the curse of the loud-speaker began chanting, more loudly this time: 'Emergency call for Dr. Kildare in Dr. Gillespie's office! Dr. Kildare, report at once to Dr. Gillespie's office...'

Lane threw out both hands and dropped them helplessly to his sides.

'Shall I answer that call?' asked Kildare.

'You've got to,' said Lane. 'I suppose Gillespie takes precedence over the rest of your work. But I wish I could have you here!'

'You don't need me,' said Kildare. 'You've got the finest pair of hands in the hospital. They don't know how to make mistakes!'

Gregory Lane took a long breath, but it seemed to do him no good.

'He's dying under my eyes,' he said, a stethoscope against the breast of Thornton. 'He's on his last legs, Kildare. What in the name of God shall I do?'

'There's no use calling on God,' said Kildare. 'The way I understand it, when the big pinch comes, a doctor has to *be* God!'

He got out of the emergency ward as he spoke.

CHAPTER EIGHT

It was a bad enough case that Kildare found waiting for him when he reached Gillespie's office, but an adrenaline injection rallied the patient so that she could be carried off to bed. And then the usual line for diagnosis began to pour in.

Time flew away on wings out of the consciousness of Kildare while various things were happening in the emergency ward. Thornton was developing the classical pressure symptoms: hardening of the arm and leg muscles on the side of the body opposite to the fracture, and a dilation of the pupil of the eye on the same side as the lesion. Lane took a spinal puncture. There was increased pressure in the spinal fluid, but no blood stain was in it. That ought to mean an extradural hemorrhage.

Lane looked with vague eyes at the nurse.

'Yes, Doctor?' she said.

'That man is dying,' he announced. 'There's nothing to save him except an operation.'

'But he's refused an operation, Doctor.'

' "In a pinch, a doctor has to *be* God," ' quoted Lane.

'What was that, Doctor?' she asked.

Lane shrugged his shoulders. He kept using her as a focal point of observation while his idea settled.

'I don't suppose that Carew would give me authority to operate?' he suggested.

'Oh, I don't think so. He's a stickler for every legal right of the patient.'

'Including the right of dying?'

He rang Carew's office. The doctor was out. It was not even known where he would be for another hour. Another hour was too long to wait.

He went back to the patient and the nurse.

'You know this hospital better than I do,' he said to the nurse. 'Is there anyone other than Carew who could authorize this operation?'

'No one would dare—I don't think anyone would dare,' she said. 'Not even Dr. Gillespie. Oh, but yes—Dr. Gillespie *could* authorize anything, I suppose.'

He rang Gillespie's office. Nurse Parker answered that he was out. He would not be returning soon. He was attending an important conference.

Gregory Lane, as he rang off, sat for a moment at the telephone with growing cold in his heart. He kept reasoning about the case, but he already knew what he would do. Of course any case was worth saving, but there was something extra about Thornton.

He went back to the dying patient.

He lifted the eyelid and glanced at the dilating pupil of the eye. He felt again the spastic hardening of the arm and leg muscles. The subconscious mind was controlling those muscles now.

He had killed seven in a row and if anything went wrong now—he would be thrown out of the hospital. No decent institution ever would take him on again.

'Order an operating room for me,' he said

to the nurse. 'Get one at once!'

'No, please! You know that he refused the operation!'

'As though a man always knew what was good for him!' said Lane. 'Order the surgery at once!'

There was not a trembling nerve in his body. The pinch had come and he was ready to play God.

Outside the surgery, Gregory Lane and the dying man passed a whole cluster of people who were there to look and make sure with their own incredulous eyes that any man dared to break the vital laws of medicine as this fellow was doing. They knew his record. His record was in their eyes as they stared on him.

In the moment when he was washing up, putting on the white gown and gloves, he kept thinking of Kildare, from whom he had received the vital impulse. There were tales about young Kildare which even the oldest men on the hospital staff told, half smiling and shaking their heads at the same time. They told, with a shudder of pleasure, how the interne had dug his toes in and resisted all authority time and again. The career of Kildare seemed to prove that a doctor can break every rule as long as he wins the game.

Now the operating table. He was looking down at the dead face of Thornton in profile as his hands started to work.

When it was ended, the heart of Thornton still beat, and without that frightful drag in it. He ought to live. There was not one chance in a thousand that he would die. Lane had him assigned to a private room and nurse—by a lucky chance on the same floor on which Mary Lamont worked. The bills could be addressed to Lane himself, until Thornton's will and ability to pay were discovered. To the doctor that case meant more than money. It was the end of bad luck. It was the end of boyhood and the commencing of maturity. The hospital still might destroy him, but it would be a long time before this work was forgotten.

CHAPTER NINE

The private nurse was a slightly damaged blonde. The cloud of glory she trailed behind her was a thick perfume that wrinkled the nose.

Mary Lamont was not three doors away when she heard a screech of fear run out into the corridor. It was the blonde special, squealing with terror.

'Don't go in!' cried the special nurse. 'He's batty. They've knocked him nutty with the operation; they've whittled the brain out of him!'

Mary Lamont got into the room in time to find Henry Thornton clambering from his bed. When she put her hands against his shoulders it was like pressing against knotty wood. There was no yield or give in him. He had looked as weak as a woman. Now he took both her wrists inside one hand and crushed them together. There was pain up to the screaming point, but she kept on smiling at him.

'They've put me in the wrong day of the week,' he said. 'I've got to get out of here. They've walled me in, you see?'

'I see,' said Mary.

'They're building the walls higher all the time. They build them out of sunlight as slippery as glass. You can't climb them. Not even an eagle could fly over them. There's only one thing to do. That's to break through. I've got to break through...'

His voice grew up to a yell. He took her by the hair of the head and put her resistlessly behind him. She held his arms.

'It's all true,' she said. 'But this is the wrong time.'

'D'you see how high they go?'

'I see how high. It makes me dizzy, looking up. We can plan it together, how to get out.'

'Are we together, you and I?'

'Yes,' she said, 'we're together.'

'If that were a lie,' he said, 'I'd have to strangle it in your throat so it couldn't get out again. It would be my *duty* to strangle it, in your throat.'

'It's not a lie,' she said.

'Don't say it so loud,' said Thornton. 'We've got to whisper this. Nobody's to hear. Life is nothing; dying is nothing. *This* is a lot more than life. You understand?'

'I understand.'

'Answer me, then. And God pity you if the answers are wrong!'

'I'll answer,' she said.

★   ★   ★

The wheelchair of Gillespie came bowling through the door of his office, propelled by Conover.

'I've brought a surprise for you, young Dr. Kildare. A father, in short.'

Old Dr. Stephen Kildare stood smiling in the doorway, his head down a bit.

'Look at the way your boy sweats, Kildare,' said Gillespie. 'Other people perspire when they work with their hands but he sweats when he uses his brain. That's because he comes from the country.'

Kildare held his father's hand a moment before he could realize that the old doctor was there.

'Yes,' Kildare admitted. 'I've never outgrown Dartford. Are you all right, Father?'

'I had to bring down Julia Cray to let some wiser heads consider her case,' said the father.

'He brought her down and put her in a different hospital. The Blair General isn't good enough for these Kildares,' said Gillespie.

'And Mother?' asked Kildare.

'She's over at the hotel. She had some shopping or something to do. Maybe she wanted to see somebody, too. I can't tell.'

'I'll be there tonight. Is Mrs. Cray very ill?'

'I've borrowed Dr. Gillespie's brain,' said old Kildare. Fragile, white-haired, slender, his manner was as quiet as that of his son, but there was no suggestion of the bulldog about him. He looked as though his way had been to bow to the storm, not stubbornly face it, as young James Kildare was wont to do. 'I borrowed the time of Dr. Gillespie, and so *he* can tell you about her.'

'No, no, old fellow,' said Gillespie. 'Tell your son something about the case ... There's going to be trouble here, Jimmy. By God, there's going to be a lot of trouble! A confounded country doctor comes down here to New York and pretends that he wants to see an internist; but all the time he has his mind made up as solid as rock!'

He grinned at Stephen Kildare, who disclaimed this attitude with eloquent gestures. 'I know him,' said the young

52

Kildare. 'Nobody pays any attention to him, here, when he roars.'

'Nobody pays any attention—that's true,' thundered Gillespie. 'I'm worn out; I'm a has-been; but go on with the case history, Stephen.'

'Julia Cray is nearly fifty, now,' said the elder Kildare. 'And recently she's developed weakness; loss of appetite, loss of weight but chiefly the weakness that makes her want to stay in bed. I've gone through the usual procedures and had her chest X-rayed. It was negative for pathology. A gastric analysis showed her markedly deficient in hydrochloric acid. These things, to me, point toward pernicious anemia. The slide of the blood doesn't give the usual picture for that disease; so I assume her case to be in a state of remission. I've been treating her accordingly.'

'Remission! Remission!' boomed Gillespie. 'He *assumes* a state of remission, and I hate to assume any state at all. What's the character of this Julia Cray?'

'She's a good woman, brave, and gentle, and faithful, and a wise mother and wife,' said Stephen Kildare. 'Perhaps it almost follows as a corollary that she is just a little foolish in certain respects? She is devoted to a nostrum, a silly herb tea which she considers medicinal.'

'And isn't it?' demanded Gillespie.

'She thinks it is keeping her alive; but you and I know that she's dying, Leonard.'

'Never mind what we know. Did you look at her tea?'

'Mere casual weeds, most of the things in it. I have had them identified, one by one,' said the elder Kildare.

'Say what you will,' said Gillespie, 'my bet is that the woman is suffering from hyperthyroidism. Too much thyroid. That's her trouble, I take it, though God knows the basal metabolism tomorrow may prove that I'm a liar!'

'Bet?' said young Kildare. 'Did you say you'd bet on it, sir?'

'Certainly!' answered Gillespie. 'I'll bet on anything. What about it, Stephen? Will you back up judgment with a little hard cash?'

'I don't pretend,' said the older Kildare, 'to have anything like your mass of experience in this or any other phase of medicine.'

'Look here, Kildare,' said Gillespie, 'a fellow that's more modest than he needs to be is almost a liar, by my reckoning. Don't pretend that you're overawed by my reputation, you Yankee hypocrite!'

'Ah, but reputation is a worker of miracles,' said the country doctor. 'Poor Julia Cray was a nervous wreck; she was already planning her own funeral but I bring her to the great Gillespie and at once she grows quiet and begins to hope.'

'Confound you, Stephen, you use me like a rattle or a nursery rhyme to amuse your patients and get their minds off themselves ... But I'm betting a dollar that it's not pernicious anemia.'

He took the bill from his pocket and flourished it violently. Old Stephen Kildare slowly drew a greenback from his pocket in turn.

'You're sure that you want to make this bet, Father?' asked the young Kildare, biting his lip to keep back the smile.

'Against Leonard Gillespie?' echoed the father. 'My dear lad. I know who Dr. Gillespie is, but if this were the Judgment Day and he were the Archangel Gabriel, and blowing his horn in my ear to prove it, I'd bet an honest dollar on an honest opinion. And my opinion is that it isn't hyperthyroidism. I'll bet on pernicious anemia against that.'

He held out the dollar bill. 'Maybe Jimmy would be the stakeholder?' he suggested.

'Ah, you're going to keep the money in the family, are you?' asked Gillespie.

The loud-speaker in the next room called loudly: 'Dr. Kildare wanted instantly in Room 412. Dr. Kildare wanted instantly in Room 412.'

Young Kildare ran from the office, still pushing the two dollar bills into his pocket.

He was still grinning a little when he stepped from the elevator on the fourth floor. It was not the first time a Kildare had ventured to oppose the ideas of the great man.

He forgot all that when he saw a cluster of frightened nurses at the door of Room 412. A slightly battered blonde nurse met him, saying: 'She called out to send for you—we've sent for Dr. Lane, too.'

'Is this his case?' exclaimed Kildare.

'And clean batty!' said the special.

Kildare opened the door softly, quickly. Thornton, his head swathed in bandages so that he looked something like a devout Mohammedan, had thrust Mary Lamont back against the wall.

He was saying: 'You lied! They've closed me into the wrong day. They've closed me in the walls like glass. And you've helped to build them high.'

She was not struggling. Kildare saw that before he got to Thornton.

'Good stuff! Good work!' he said to Mary Lamont, and then put his arm around the sick man. At the touch the strength of the mania melted out of Thornton and he sagged helplessly as Kildare lifted him back into bed.

He kept saying: 'Who is it? Who's here?' and straining his eyes as though he were staring into a thick fog.

'I'm Kildare, and I'm here to talk it all

over, quietly . . . Get Lane!' he added over his shoulder to Mary Lamont.

The door was open and a dozen entranced faces were looking in at the crisis. Mary Lamont went out and closed the door after her.

Inside the room Kildare was saying: 'Now you're thinking ahead, Thornton. You're thinking ahead to Friday.'

The word opened and half-cleared the misted, weary eyes of the sick man.

The insistent, gentle voice of Kildare said, with hypnotic monotony: 'Friday—noon— noon—Friday—and what's happening, Thornton?'

'I'm there,' answered Thornton, smiling. 'I'm there, and it's all happiness, forever.'

'What is it? What's the happiness?' asked Kildare.

'Forever! Happiness forever!' said Thornton.

His voice died out. He fell asleep, still smiling, and his hand relaxed in the assuring grasp of Kildare, who now stood up. Lane and Mary Lamont were standing in the room, watching, silent.

'How do you manage it, Kildare?' asked Gregory Lane. 'Hypnotize them, some way?'

Kildare smiled faintly. He went over to Mary.

'That was a good job you did,' he said. He took her hand. 'That was as good a job as I ever saw ... Thornton was about to manhandle her,' he explained to Lane, 'and she kept her eyes on him and didn't struggle. She was as quiet as a stone. Quiet, and still smiling. It was a great job!'

'I've been a fool,' said Lane. 'I should have had a man, an attendant, in here. Mary, were you hurt?'

'Not much,' she said, rubbing a bruised wrist.

'Stay out of this room!' commanded Lane.

'No, she's all right,' said Kildare.

'D'you mean to say that you'd let her risk herself in here again?' asked Lane.

'Why not?' asked Kildare. 'A girl's not worth a rap if you encourage her to show the white feather. There're plenty of yellow rats. This one is different. Let's keep her different.'

Thornton suddenly groaned and sat up in the bed.

'I'm coming as fast ...' he began, 'I'll be there ... wait for me...'

He started to get out of bed. Kildare went to him.

'Dr. Lane!' said a nurse from the hall, pushing open the door. 'Dr. Carew wants you.'

'Good luck!' whispered Mary Lamont.

CHAPTER TEN

The justice of Dr. Carew, as head of the Blair General Hospital, was as quick as a knifestroke and often as sharp. But he conducted his trials of offenders with a certain air of legal procedure. When he put Gregory Lane on the carpet, he said: 'Dr. Lane, I believe that I have the facts of this case firmly in hand. I had a definite attitude toward you yesterday, and I should have acted on it. But I allowed another opinion to dissuade me. I regret that I permitted myself to listen to that persuasion!'

He made a pause, here. He considered young Gregory Lane from head to foot.

'You came here with a promising background,' said Carew. 'Otherwise I never would have considered such a young man for a post as neurosurgeon. After your recent arrival, you have had a series of strokes of—bad luck? Seven men have died under your knife. Medical accidents? It is beyond accident, in my opinion. It has reached such a point that I feel guilty of manslaughter— because I've permitted you to work in this hospital.'

He made another pause.

'If you're waiting for me to say something,' said Lane, 'I may as well tell you now what I

59

think.'

'Ah, you think, do you?' asked Carew. 'A dangerous thing for a surgeon to think too much. A dangerous thing, if a thought gets between his knife and the incision he's making. But I'm interested—what is it you think?'

'I think that there was nothing wrong with the operation.'

'Ah ha! Nothing wrong with it? A patient goes mad under your knife, but you *think* that there was nothing wrong with the operation?'

'I definitely know that if the same case came to me again, I would follow the same procedure. I would operate.'

Actually, there was not a word that came to the mind of Carew. He was silent because he was stunned.

Finally the pale lips of Gregory Lane parted. He said: 'You can come to the point, Dr. Carew. I'm dismissed from the hospital service, I presume?'

'You may presume what you please; but I would like, in the first place, to open my mind to you.'

'I am here to listen, sir,' said Gregory Lane.

'I have the full details of your procedure before, and during the operation. You dared to operate on a man who distinctly had refused our medical assistance! That is true,

I believe?'

'That is obviously true,' said Dr. Lane.

'There was only one authority in this hospital that could have ventured to give you that authority. Perhaps *I* might have delegated it to you. Or perhaps Leonard Gillespie might have taken it upon him to set the work forward. But, so far as I know, you worked without the slightest authorization.'

Rage, even before the expected answer, swelled the jowls of Carew.

'Without the slightest authorization,' agreed Dr. Lane.

Carew got up from his chair to deliver a violent denunciation and dismissal speech. But there was a large stratum of justice in his being and he knew that a good judge should not speak in passion. That was why he said: 'That will be all for the present.'

'Very well, sir,' said Lane, and turned to the door.

'My earnest endeavor,' said Carew, 'shall be to think this through without passion. I shall continue to look into the affair. I shall have a further message to communicate to you within the hour, I trust. Good-by, Dr. Lane.'

Lane went out.

He took a look in at Room 412. Mary Lamont was standing close to the door, which was slightly ajar to give a better current of air.

'How is he now?' asked Lane.

'Dr. Kildare is in there still,' she said, 'and he has Mr. Thornton quiet again.'

'What is it that Kildare does to them?'

'No one knows. But sick people always trust him. They feel him helping them up the hill. But he can't get what he wants from Mr. Thornton.'

'He wants to know what that deadline means? What noon Friday means to Thornton?'

'That's it. But Thornton hasn't told. Not yet. Either he thinks he's locked forever in the wrong day of the week, or else he imagines that Friday has come, and there's nothing but happiness.'

Kildare came out of the room, stepping softly.

'He's sleeping,' he said, 'and the sleep isn't all barbital. Be quiet, Mary, when you go to him.'

'How is he?' asked Lane.

'He's the same. Noon, on Friday—noon, on Friday—and he's locked into the wrong day of the week,' murmured Kildare, absently.

He went off down the hall, walking slowly, almost stopped by his thoughts from time to time.

Gregory Lane, looking after him, said: 'It's hard to guess how a fellow like that could mean much to a girl; but if he *did* come to mean anything, I don't see how she could give a rap about any other man.'

'Why do you say that?' asked Mary Lamont, her voice sharp with interest.

'Because women are practical creatures with an eye to the main chance,' said Lane, 'and there's nothing small about Kildare. No wooden chairs for him. He wants the golden throne. The little things don't matter to him. He doesn't even see them. He doesn't know whether his shoes are shined or not; he doesn't know whether his feet are dry or wet; he doesn't know what street he's walking; he only knows whether or not he's headed in the right direction. Isn't that the secret of him?'

'Is it?' she asked. 'I don't know.'

'The little things—damn them! They wreck most of us. They make the difference between fame and, say, just hard cash. And the little things don't exist, for Kildare.'

'You say nice things about Dr. Kildare, but you don't like him.'

'What makes you think that?'

'Because your voice is hard when you speak about him.'

'I'll tell you this: He's the stuff I'd like to have for a friend. But there's something about me that offends him.'

'Really?'

'You know the straight way he has of looking at people?'

'Oh, yes, I know!'

'Well, he won't look at me, if he can avoid it.'

'But I've heard him say that he admires you.'

'He admires a pair of surgeon's hands, not me. And you can't be very fond of a fellow who's adverse to you.'

A voice sounded vaguely from 412. Lane stepped close to the door.

'The wrong day—' said the sleepy utterance. 'They've locked me inside the wrong day...'

The words drawled away into sleep again.

CHAPTER ELEVEN

Now that the interview with Gregory Lane was over, Carew took up the witnesses in rapid succession. He already knew the burden of the testimony which most of them had to give, but he wanted to have it freshly in mind before he delivered a judgment that already was hardening in his mind.

The frightened little nurse from the emergency ward stood before him, saying: 'I knew it was wrong; I begged him not to do it; I knew it was wrong...'

There was the ambulance driver and the interne who had picked up the accident call.

They described the scene of the crime, the apparent state of the injury. There was the X-ray man with his picture. There was even the orderly who had pushed the stretcher up to the operating room.

Finally, there was Kildare. No matter how grim the mind of Carew might be, he relaxed a little when Gillespie's assistant came into the office.

'You've been here before, and on a slightly different basis, Doctor,' said Carew, smiling. 'There even have been times when this floor was a hard place for you to stand. Eh?'

'Very hard,' said Kildare, and smiled a bit, also.

'That was before your value to the hospital became so apparent,' went on Carew. 'And any man who has value to the hospital, has intimate personal value to me!'

All of Carew's strokes were apt to be like this. Whether he gave a criticism or a compliment, he leaned his whole weight behind his words.

Kildare murmured something. What he said hardly mattered, for Carew was sweeping forward on his genial way.

'Today, Doctor,' he said, 'I simply want a word from you about the unfortunate case of Henry Thornton—the case which the new neurosurgeon handled—I refer to Dr. Gregory Lane. And I believe you saw the patient who was forced into an unbalanced state of mind by the—shall I call it unlucky?—work of Dr. Lane.'

'I beg your pardon, sir,' said Kildare. 'I believe the patient was already showing signs of schizophrenia before the operation.'

'Already?' exclaimed Carew, shocked out of his good-natured flow of verbiage. 'Before what?'

'Before the operation, sir.'

'Extraordinary,' said Carew, 'I had thought certainly—in fact it had not occurred to me that any other cause—'

'Did you ask Dr. Lane about it?' asked Kildare gently.

'Perhaps not. The—ah—the general report indicated nothing unbalanced previous to the operation ... Kildare, what was the exact nature of the expression of this schizophrenia?'

'Can you imagine a man who would consider that any date line is more important than life or death, sir?'

'Hardly. But it's barely conceivable.'

'His entire expression was that of a man who has been under a great tension for a long time. For five years I believe that the strain was being put upon him. Finally, he began to crumble. He was already crumbling, I think, before he reached the hospital.'

'This is all assumption, mere assumption,' said Carew, darkly.

'Yes, sir,' agreed Kildare, 'it's chiefly that.'

'The status of Dr. Lane undoubtedly would be much better if the condition of Thornton were not referable to the operation which he performed. Of course that leaves out a still more important consideration: That he operated without the permission of the patient.'

'That was the refusal of a patient mentally unsound.'

'Ha?' cried Carew. 'Unsound? Well, in that case it was absolutely essential that the permission of a near relative should be obtained.'

'We still haven't even a home address for Thornton,' said Kildare. 'How could relatives be reached?'

'Which makes it all the more absolutely decisive that Lane should not have touched Thornton without advice from me—or from Gillespie, at least.'

'But of course, in a certain way, Dr. Lane was under the impression that he had authorization from Dr. Gillespie.'

'What's this, Kildare?' demanded Carew. 'What the devil is this that you're saying to me?'

'There wasn't time to go into the details,' said Kildare. 'Dr. Lane understood from what I said that Dr. Gillespie actually had recommended an immediate operation.'

'That Gillespie had ... but I've had Lane

in here saying he had no authorization from anyone whatever! What am I to make of this?'

'A man like Dr. Lane is built along rather large lines,' said Kildare thoughtfully. 'I suppose he didn't want to dump the blame on my shoulders.'

'You actually advised the operation and let him feel that Gillespie was speaking through you?'

'I'm afraid that was about it.'

'Your shoulders, I dare say,' said Carew, 'are broad enough to bear much greater burdens than blame like this?'

Kildare was silent. The anger of Carew grew until a vein swelled visibly in his forehead.

'I've told Gillespie that he was wrong, damned wrong, to let a boy, a mere youngster, act as his mouthpiece so often. And now we have a fine result from it?' cried Carew.

He got up from his chair and walked the floor, hastily, taking quick turns back and forth.

'I'm not going to let myself get out of hand about this,' he said. 'In the past you've had values, young Dr. Kildare. But perhaps they were based too largely on certain traits of stubborn independence. I want to point out that we cannot...'

He choked himself.

'I have to see Gillespie,' he finished. 'Will you ask him to come up here?'

Kildare left the office and returned to Gillespie with the message.

'I'm going to ask the board of directors for a gag that will fit the mouth of that catfish, that Carew,' roared Gillespie, and let Conover wheel him out toward the elevators.

The interrupted line commenced to flow in on Kildare, as it did sometimes with hardly an interruption for days at a time, in obedience to that famous brass plate above the door on which was engraved the words: 'Dr. Leonard Gillespie, hours 12 A.M. to 12 A.M.' It would have been a dry jest, from another man. It was cold fact, coming from Gillespie.

Then Gillespie himself came back and cleared the office with one of his roars.

'Did you really do it, Jimmy?' he asked, when they were alone.

'What, sir?'

'Set up this fellow Thornton for operation by—er—by using my name?'

'Yes, sir!'

'You actually made Lane think that I was behind the idea?'

Kildare said nothing.

'It's queer,' said Gillespie. 'I'm not fool enough to think that I know any man, really; but this time you've surprised me. You surprised Carew, too, but not very much.'

Kildare began to say that he was sorry. Gillespie cut him short by remarking: 'A fellow like Carew is a blessing to the institution he heads and a curse to a good many other things. He's an executive first, a damned good doctor second. But he always thinks that he's a general.'

'He's going to give me the limit?' asked Kildare.

'He was torn in two directions,' said Gillespie. 'You've done so much for the hospital that he's grateful, he's almost affectionate. On the other hand you've done so much for the hospital that you're an outstanding figure even as an interne. It's like this: If a private disobeys orders, he can be sent to the guardhouse. But if a general officer disobeys the high command, he's cashiered.'

'I understand,' said Kildare.

'You have from here to Friday for something more than understanding,' answered Gillespie. 'You have that time to do something about it!'

'You managed to get that much delay?'

'Never mind what I did. The question is: What are we going to do, Jimmy?'

He gathered his shaggy, white brows over his eyes and folded his hands together, backs up.

'There's another question first,' said Kildare. 'Is there anything that I possibly *could* do to straighten it out?'

'It's not simply "you"; it's "we", you fool!'

'Yes, sir.'

'Why couldn't some other young jackass in the place have had the idea? But no, it had to be *my* boy.'

Kildare, staring at him, bit his lip. He did not speak for the moment because there was no room in his throat for words.

'Friday the board of directors is meeting. And the case of young Dr. Kildare comes up, as it came up once before. Only then you were just a young fool who broke the rules and now you're a reprobate, dyed-in-the-wool, who has formed the rotten habit of doing as he pleases, regardless of the higher-ups. Friday is the day when your head goes off, then. And now, Jimmy, we put our heads together. State the case to me, first of all.'

Kildare said: 'Dr. Lane performs an authorized operation that produces insanity in the patient; it's discovered that the fault is mine, after all. So I get the gallows.'

'Let's ask the right questions first, and then maybe we'll get the answers. What could be done to take the curse off?'

'If I could *prove* that the insanity existed before the operation, that would take the curse off.'

'It's hard to prove things like that—to a

71

Carew? But if the insanity could be removed, or seem to be removed? What are your cards, Kildare? What have you got in the pack or up your sleeve? If there's a fine, clean, straightforward way, we'll use it. If not, we'll deal off the bottom of the deck.'

'Well, a shock was what started him raving. It brought the disease on him with a rush.'

'And if we can give him another shock—a happy shock—if we prove to him that the strain he was under before the operation is gone—if we clear the whole emotional air of his life—you think that it might bring him back to normalcy?'

'There's a ghost of a chance, perhaps.'

'That's better than nothing. We can't ask for the world with a fence around it. We want a chance to fight. That's all. A ghost of a chance is a damned sight better than no chance at all. *Hamlet's* father was only a ghost, Jimmy. But he's still a force in our minds. So now we do what?'

'We find out what it is that he had to meet on Friday at noon.'

'And then meet it for him?'

'Yes, sir.'

'And bring him back the results?'

'Yes, sir.'

'And with Thornton restored to his wits, even Carew will have to admit that the operation was a fine thing?'

'Yes, sir.'

'So that Carew can damn you black and blue for encouraging the operation but he can't quite take off your head?'

'I hope that it may turn out that way,' said Kildare.

'What do you do first?'

'I try to be a detective, and of course I'm not one.'

'Not a detective? Confound you, make yourself into one, then! A doctor has to be a nurse, a cook, a family lawyer, a mother, a father, a rat-killer, and why in the name of God can't he go a step backward, or forward, and be a detective?'

'I'm going to tackle it,' said Kildare.

'Then get out of my sight and start now. Wait a minute. There's another thing involved here. Do you have no pangs of conscience about using my name to Lane, as you did?'

'No, sir.'

'You mean that you'd do it again, without any permission?'

'Yes, sir.'

'Damned impudence, I call it,' said Gillespie, and, 'Well, get on with you! I'd disown you if you hadn't done exactly that.'

CHAPTER TWELVE

In the clothes of Henry Thornton there had been a pair of soft-lead draughting pencils, twenty odd dollars, a good, big pocketknife, cigarettes, a lighter, two handkerchiefs, an addressed envelope without the sender's name and without contents. That was all. Even the address was not in handwriting. It had been typed. There was not a trace of a laundry mark even. The underwear and shirts apparently had been new-bought. The clothes were the product of a wholesale tailoring firm whose suits were sold in fifty metropolitan stores. There was only a bit of reddish mud high inside the angle of heel and sole on one of the shoes. Kildare gloomily scraped it off, put it into a twist of paper. He did not feel like a detective, but like a fool.

The Museum of Natural History in Manhattan is one of those places where people take their children to admire prehistoric skeletons. As a matter of fact there is hardly a physical phase of life that is not touched on and illustrated in the Museum. The whole process in the Museum is so pictorial that when Kildare took his paper twist of dry mud to Professor McGregor, that bright little old man at once pulled out a chart which, like a crazy quilt of a thousand colors, showed the soils around New York, and the rock strata underlying them, or outcropping through them. Professor McGregor, after crumbling the mud to a fine dust, segregated some tiny particles of stone which he placed under a microscope.

He kept whistling as he worked and finally he looked up to the earnest face of Kildare with eyes that shone like polished lenses.

'Unless the stone is imported stuff, I think I have the place,' said Professor McGregor. 'Ever driven out from the East Side toward Westchester?'

'Yes.'

'Well, over to the right, as you drive north, you see some land, somewhat broken, so that it looks like a low range of hills, almost. Two chances out of three, that's your district. Look, here's the map. You see this pink patch? Somewhere inside that district. It's not very large.'

Kildare went back to the hospital and looked up his friend, the ambulance driver with the numb, unconscious face.

'Tell me,' said Kildare, 'where I can get the cheapest drive-yourself car in town. Do you know, Joe?'

'There's none of them cheap enough. Not for you, Doc,' said Joe Weyman. 'But me brother-in-law has a little bus that needs borrowing.'

'You mean I could rent it from him?' asked Kildare.

'You mean, could he rent a sock in the chin?' demanded Weyman. 'How could he take money from you? When d'you want it?'

'Now.'

'Right this afternoon?'

'Yes.'

'And me with my time off starting in half an hour!' said Weyman. '*That's* luck, ain't it? You can close your eyes and catch up on some sleep; I'll do the driving.'

So they started within the hour, with Weyman tooling the car with a sort of reckless precision through the traffic.

The rain came down in a steady, misting fall. But at last they came toward the low-lying hills.

'Pull up to that lunch wagon,' said Kildare.

He went in alone and got a cup of coffee. When he was half through with it, he asked the waiter: 'You know a man named Henry Thornton who lives out here?'

'Sure I know Thornbury,' said the waiter. 'He's the guy with the big green house on the hill over by...'

'Shut up, rummy,' said a big young man who was trying to get half his ham and eggs into his mouth at a bite.

'Not Thornbury, you poor mug. Thornton

is the guy he asked about.'

He was still looking his reproof as he went on: 'This here Thornton you wanta know about, is he thirty something and lives alone and looks it?'

'You might describe him that way,' said Kildare, delighted. 'Does he live alone?'

'Yeah. He ain't married.'

'How do I find Thornton's house?' asked Kildare.

'That's easy. You go up here to the top of the hill, turn left, and it's three houses down.'

Kildare went up to the top of the hill, turned left, and asked Weyman to wait at the corner.

'Do you mind, Joe?' he asked.

'Whatta ya mean mind?' asked Weyman. 'But you know where you're going?'

'I think I know, all right.'

'You kinda make me nervous when you start strange places all by yourself.'

'I can take care of myself pretty well, Joe.'

'Yeah, sure, sure. But if you had a good right cross up your sleeve it would take care of you a lot better. I'm gunna teach you, some of these fine days.'

CHAPTER THIRTEEN

Darkness had descended and many of the houses had lights turned on. Kildare, on the front porch, rang the bell, listened to the echo of it inside the place, and studied the jagged crack that streaked across the face of the adjoining window. He tried the window and when he found it locked he broke the glass and opened it. Then he stepped inside. He closed the window. With a burning match he found the electric switch and turned on the lights. He stood in a hall.

There was a living room at the right, so bright and cheerful that he thought for a moment the sky must have cleared but this was merely the effect of the gay covers on the furniture. The gaiety was a first impression that did not last. There was dust on the table. Cigarette butts littered the hearth, and a book fallen open, face down beside the couch, had crunched its pages into a tangle of confusion.

Back of the living room, which was unusually large for such a small house, he stepped into the kitchen. The sink was filled with unwashed pans. The water in them had begun to rust the iron in places; the queer, sick odor of rust was all through the room.

In a dining alcove he saw the remains of a

breakfast, a cup half-filled with coffee, with a scum of soured milk on top of it, and a piece of toast as hard as wood.

Forward from the kitchen a small study with a tall north light opened from the living room. A smell of old, crusted pipes was in it. Some shelves on one side held books on art and a number of sketchbooks, as well. On the drawing board which faced the high window was a bit of purely commercial stuff such as magazines or even newspapers use to illustrate new fashions.

He looked over the room again, standing in the center of it. For him, the ghost of Henry Thornton was emerging in the house.

A sighing sound came to him from the front of the house. A fallen bit of paper rattled on the floor of the studio, and then was still. It was as though a door had been opened and shut again, somewhere. Kildare blinked and took a quick breath; then he made his feet carry him through the living room. In the hall a tall figure of a man waited at the foot of the stairs. It moved, and turned into the frowning face of Joe Weyman.

'Well, Joe?' he asked.

'I broke orders, Doc,' said Weyman. 'I had to. I heard the tinkle of that glass breaking and I just had to come in an' join you. If you take a trip up the river for burglary, I might as well go along.'

'I didn't hear the window raised. How did

79

you come in?'

'Through the door. I got a little lock-persuader, here.' He showed a small bit of steel, like a section of hard spring. 'Doc, d'you need *all* of these here lights to show the world where we're having our fun?'

'We need light,' said Kildare. He sat down and started smoking a cigarette. 'Go look through the lower part of the house and tell me what you see, when you come back.'

'Lookat—I found this near the door,' said Weyman. He held out a slip of paper on which was written in a swift, strong hand:

'DARLING:
I lost my key and couldn't get in; but now I'll find it and come.
Nelly.'

'Him and Nelly, I bet they have high times,' said Weyman.

'It doesn't fit,' answered Kildare, and crumbling the paper impatiently, he dropped it into his pocket. 'Go look around and tell me what you find.'

In two minutes Weyman was back.

'Kind of sloppy guy. No?' he asked.

'See anything worthwhile?'

'This guy don't know nothing about women,' said Weyman. 'See the mugs he was drawing, in there?'

'Let's go upstairs,' said Kildare.

80

There were two bedrooms, one obviously for guests, and one bathroom. They went through the bathroom into the guest room, first. The door of it was so jammed that Weyman had to give it his shoulder. They turned on the lights.

'What's the funny smell in the air, Doc?'

'Dust,' said Kildare. 'This fellow Thornton has no friends. There's been no one in this guest room for a long, long time. That's why the door stuck, Joe. It simply hadn't been opened and the heat of a couple of summers gummed the paint together.'

He pointed it out at the edges of the door. Weyman said nothing as they went back into the master bedroom. There was a good thick rug on the floor and a bed that sat low on the floor with a stool for a bedside table with a short lamp on it. On the walls were varnished Medici prints of the Duchess of Modena and Rembrandt's Knight with a Spear. There was also an oil portrait of a redheaded girl in a green dress. She was no beauty, but she had a good smile and a fine, straight pair of eyes. The telephone, oddly enough, stood on the chest of drawers. A single number was written down on the pad beside it. There was a tall mirror against one wall, and opposite it was a closet containing a few suits of clothes.

There was a small desk beside the closet door, with a clean blotter on top of it.

Kildare pulled the blotter out from its frame and turned it over. It was spotted with ink blottings and with absent-minded designs in pencil.

'What's on there that you wanta know, Doc?' asked Weyman.

'A lot of unhappiness,' said Kildare.

'How come?'

'Wasted time,' he said.

He went over to the picture of the girl and pulled it out from the wall. The paper behind it was only slightly less faded than the rest of the paper in the room. That behind the other pictures was far darker and richer.

'How is this, Weyman?' he asked. 'He painted this picture six or seven years ago—or maybe only five. And yet he hung it only a short time ago.'

'How can you tell, Doc ... Ah, you mean the paper's faded a lot where it hangs.'

'It was hanging there for a while,' interpreted Kildare, 'then it was taken down, remained down for years, and finally was put up again.'

'Kind of cuckoo, ain't he?' said Weyman.

'I don't know,' said Kildare. 'Go and stand in front of that mirror.'

'How's this? I look damn fine to me, Doc.'

'Stand closer.'

'Here I am, touching the glass.'

'Somebody stood still closer, however,' remarked Kildare, staring at the rug.

'Nobody *could* stand closer.'

'The rug's worn,' said Kildare. 'Feet seem to have walked right through that mirror. Can we move it?'

That was easily done, and behind the mirror appeared a door. Weyman's bit of steel spring was used on the lock which gave at last with a small squeak, like the shrill of a mouse. Inside, they found a closet with a few women's clothes in it.

Kildare reached into the closet and brought out a wisp of spiderweb.

'She doesn't come very often, Joe,' he said. He took out a green dress and shook dust out of it. 'Not for about five years.'

'Five years? Where's the date?'

'This was the fashion, five and six years ago. This is the dress he painted her in.'

'Come on, Doc! You mean that?'

'See the bit of red peasant embroidery? It's the same dress, all right.'

'Then what's it mean? Why's he hang the picture on the wall and cover up the closet where her duds hang?'

Kildare went to the telephone and rang the number that was written on the pad.

'Mahoney speakin'!' said a great voice.

'This is Henry Thornton,' said Kildare.

'Thornton? Thornton? You mean that you're *Mister* Thornton? ... Hey, Nelly!'

Kildare sighed.

Presently a rich brogue was saying: 'Is it

83

you, Mr. Thornton? Is it you, darling? I was there, the more fool me, without me key. But I'll be back tomorrow and long before Saturday I'll have the house shining. And the new slip-covers will be ready. If only I can get the other bed out of the attic; there's hardly *that* much room for me and it to come down the stairs together! But don't have a worry in your darling head, will you?'

After Kildare rang off, he said, 'Now, let's try to find letters, Joe. Letters of any kind. I'll go through this desk. You go through the downstairs.' But there was hardly a letter, and not a one that gave even a hint to Kildare.

CHAPTER FOURTEEN

Kildare said to Gillespie, an hour or more later: 'Thornton was married to a woman he loved. Something went wrong; I don't know what. She left him. After a while, he took it so hard that he couldn't stand the pain of seeing her picture on the wall.'

'Bah!' said Gillespie. 'What sort of a thin-skinned rummy is this Thornton?'

'A painter,' said Kildare.

'I've no use for them,' said Gillespie. 'Poets and painters and the whole lot, I've no use for them!'

Kildare said: 'He couldn't stand the pain of seeing her picture on the wall. So he took it down. But not long ago, not very long ago, he heard from her. He had been living like a hermit, brooding, I suppose, without friends, seeing practically no one, doing work that he despised. But now he hears from his wife. Suddenly his life opens. He has a great shock of hope. He is going to meet her, some place. I don't know the place—I only know that the time was to be Friday, at noon ... He was going to meet her and bring her home; there was to be a new start for them, probably ... At least, he'd arranged to have the house in good shape for Saturday.'

'You met somebody who knows Thornton?'

'I got into his house; it had a lot to say. But it couldn't tell me *where* he intended to meet that wife of his. That's what I've got to find. They have a right to belong to one another. I have to bring her to him ... They have the right...'

'What's your next step, young Dr. Kildare?'

'I don't know. Sit down and think, I suppose.'

'Have you got time to sit down?'

'I've got to *make* time.'

'How d'you make time, young man?'

'The way you do ... by trying to be sure before I go ahead.'

'That's right. If you're going to swing an axe, be sure you hit the line. What's your line here?'

'To make Thornton tell me where to find her.'

'How can you *make* a madman talk sense?'

'I don't know. Only have a vague idea.'

'Your idea isn't vague at all. And it's scaring hell out of you,' said Gillespie.

Kildare lifted both hands and pushed them up across his face, pressing hard, as though the flesh were numb.

'Jimmy!' roared Gillespie.

'Yes, sir?'

'You've been a damned fool before. I forbid you to be a damned fool again!'

Kildare said nothing. He kept seeing his new idea and shrinking from it.

'You're as stubborn as your father,' said Gillespie. 'Confound him, he *insists* that it's pernicious anemia that's killing Julia Cray...'

Kildare went out. Gillespie, his mind returning to the first part of their conversation, shouted suddenly after him, but he pretended not to hear. In the corridor beyond, he ran into old Molly Byrd. With young internes her manner was hardly less autocratic than that of Gillespie.

'Young man, you've finally been able to do something worth while,' she said.

'Has Dr. Gillespie seen Carson?' he asked.

86

'Yes. Didn't you know?'

'I forgot to ask.'

'*Forgot?* Is there something bigger than Gillespie in your life, just now?'

'Molly, what did Carson say about Gillespie?'

'He says more than a person could hope—more even than you and I could hope. If Leonard will give himself even normal rest, normal food, and let the X-rays work to stop the *gallop* of the disease, we might have him ... much longer...'

'Years?' begged Kildare, suddenly big with excitement.

'No. Months,' said Molly Byrd, sadly.

'And who knows what might happen, if there are months and months?' said Kildare.

'You mean that new things are being discovered?'

'Of course they are. Any day there may be the great discovery that will wipe cancer out of the world!'

'Oh, Jimmy, there *may* be; may there not?'

'There *will* be, Molly, because there *has* to be.'

'You're only a liar, and a young liar, at that,' said Molly Byrd, with tears in her eyes.

'Molly, there's a Dr. Borodin...'

'Of course there is. He's one of my boys. And a damned *bad* boy, in the beginning.'

'I want to talk with him.'

'You're the funny one, digging and prying

into all the dark corners where the dirt is,' said the Byrd, 'but you'll get nothing out of Dick Borodin now.'

'Why not?'

'The poor man has no mind for any but one thing: Insulin shock for schizophrenics.'

'I want to see him.'

'You can't see him. He's closed up like a monk in a monastery.'

'Would he talk on the telephone?'

'If I told him to, maybe.'

'You're going to tell him to.'

'He wouldn't talk except to some great man—or maybe to me, Jimmy.'

'You're going to introduce me on the telephone as a distinguished doctor, Molly.'

'I am *not!*'

'Molly,' said Kildare, putting his arm around her, 'it's for a good cause.'

'There's no cause good enough to lie for.'

'There is, though,' said Kildare.

'Well,' said Molly, 'maybe you *are* distinguished. If there's such a thing as borrowing light, you've taken enough from Leonard Gillespie to begin to shine a bit, a small bit, in a very dark night. Come along with me!'

When Kildare had finished that telephone call, there seemed no breath left in him. He got out on the street but there wasn't enough air for him even there. He went to the hotel where his mother and father were staying.

They gave him the calmness of perfect faith and affection. They were the only human beings for whom he never could be wrong. Blind, unseeing eyes they seemed to him. His father talked about Julia Cray.

'Gillespie's a great man,' said old Kildare, 'but there are a few troubles with these hospital diagnosticians. They never get to know their patients well enough. We've put poor Julia Cray on a low salt diet, now. But mark my word, there will be a blasted crisis before long, and then we'll all see by the low blood count that pernicious anemia is what she has. Hang onto those two dollars, Jimmy, because I intend to have the great Gillespie's money on this deal. I'm going to frame that dollar bill and hang it in my office. It'll be more than a diploma to me!'

They had dinner in the hotel room. Then Kildare restlessly started to leave. His mother came with him down the hall toward the elevator.

'What is it now?' she asked.

'I've got to get out in the air,' said Kildare. 'I can't breathe—I can't get a full breath.'

'I know,' she answered. 'That happens when the heart is stopping.'

'The heart?' he asked.

'With grief, Jimmy, or anxiety.'

He nodded. The elevator opened clanging doors. He waved it on and walked back with her down the hall. She was a dumpy woman with too much chin and fat in the eyelids that made her eyes seem small. Sometimes it seemed that her husband had married a scrub woman. But there was a beauty about her, sometimes, when she spoke.

'Suppose that there were two men and a woman you had to think about. The happiness of all three of them, and the sanity of one of them—and the only way to work is to take a chance with life and death?'

'How could a woman tell,' she answered, 'unless she loved all three of them?'

'That's true,' he said. 'A woman couldn't tell.'

'I've seen your father facing problems like that,' she said softly, 'and it's the only time in our lives when I've been able to do nothing. He has to go off by himself like a prophet into a wilderness; he has to retire and eat the pain like bread. But when he comes out, he seems to know, just as surely as though God has told him.'

When he left her, he kept thinking of that phrase: Eating pain; except that it seemed that it was he who was being devoured.

When he was down on the street again there still was no air for *his* breathing.

CHAPTER FIFTEEN

Gillespie's line, that night, did not stop until nearly four in the morning. Kildare went into his own inner office, put some material into a medical kit, and passed back through the main office where Gillespie had stretched himself on the couch and seemed sound asleep. His face, his whole body, sagged with exhaustion.

Kildare went out of the office. On the fourth floor, he met Mary Lamont. She was on night duty but she kept the freshness and the verve of the day.

'Something wrong?' she asked.

'I want you right now. I'm going into 412.'

'To Thornton?'

'Yes.'

'Oh, has Gregory Lane ordered some special treatment for Thornton?'

He considered her for a moment but left that remark unanswered.

'Come to 412 in a half hour,' he said. 'I may be needing a nurse with a good pair of hands and no tongue at all.'

She looked hard at him; he turned and went off down the hall. She kept watch from a vantage point after he disappeared into 412. A moment later the special nurse came out looking decidedly odd.

'That young interne—what's his name?' she asked. It was no longer the dizzy blonde who took care of Thornton but a formidable old warhorse.

'Dr. Kildare,' explained Mary.

'He's a nut!' said the special. 'He told me to go and have myself a sleep—*he'll* watch Thornton.'

'He'll do what he says. Why don't you have the sleep?' asked Mary.

'Me? It ain't professional,' said the special. 'I'm going to be looking into this funny business. I don't like it.'

'Don't bother Dr. Kildare,' Mary warned her. 'He's Dr. Gillespie's assistant.'

'That young mug?' cried the special.

'That young mug,' Mary assured her.

'Things are going to the devil around here,' said the special and went off down the hall.

Mary Lamont, half an hour later, paused at the door of 412 and heard strange noises. She looked in and saw Henry Thornton babbling with an idiot's loose face. Kildare looked up and waved her away.

'Come back in half an hour,' he directed.

'I'll be back.'

He stared an instant at his immobile patient before he turned to her again.

'You look rather chipper, Mary.'

'I suppose I've had good news,' she said.

'About what?'

'About a marriage.'

'Yours? Lane?' he asked.

'Oh, Jimmy, pretend that it upsets you a little, please!'

'Of course it upsets me,' he said, but again his glance left her and studied the face of Thornton.

'You don't care a rap,' she told him.

He looked up at her in a silence which, somehow, dissolved her anger utterly.

'I'll be seeing you here in about half an hour, Mary?' he asked.

'Yes, in a half hour,' she said.

'Has that special been hanging around?' he asked.

'No. What did you do to her?'

'Sent her away. I don't want her. She's suspicious, Mary; and she may come prying back here again.'

'Well, what could she find out?'

'Enough to break me up into little pieces.'

'Jimmy! What are you doing to Thornton?'

'I want a nurse with a head and two hands and no damned tongue at all,' said Kildare.

She backed out of the room, fighting herself to keep from exclamations.

Half an hour later still, she found Henry Thornton stretched in coma, his hands thrown up above his head. Beside the bed Kildare crouched on a chair like a poisoner at the place of crime. He turned to Mary a white face, greasy with sweat.

'What is it, Jimmy?' she asked. 'Please, please tell me!'

He said nothing. She went to the foot of the bed and looked at the chart. There was no indication that special medication had been given. Whatever Kildare had done, he had left no indication of it. That could mean any sort of trouble, if the head of the institution chose to be particular. But she was afraid to ask questions.

Kildare kept looking up at her without speaking. He had given one hand to the grip of Thornton and the clutch of the sick man was fixed rigidly on it. His other hand took the pulse.

'Is he in a fit?' said Mary Lamont.

'He's minus the brain of Homo sapiens,' said Kildare.

She waited for words that would make sense.

'You've dreamed yourself back to childhood in your sleep, haven't you?' asked Kildare. 'Thornton is doing more than that. He's dreamed himself back to the infancy of the race. The muscles he's using now are the ones that an ape needs when it's climbing trees.'

She stared at the clutching hands of Thornton.

'Jimmy,' she whispered, 'do you know what you're doing to him?'

Kildare said: 'Don't ask questions. Keep

94

looking in. I may need you.'

That was about five o'clock. Obediently she forced her feet out of the room. Every half hour she returned.

It was like taking a silent part in a murder. Each time she looked at Thornton, she knew that the sick man was a long step nearer death, and still Kildare crouched there with his stethoscope and a flashlight, watching, lifting an eyelid of Thornton now and then and flashing the light upon it. She could not recognize the thing Kildare had become. More than once she heard, from 412, noises that seemed to come from the throat of a beast. A horrible memory came back out of her childhood of ghostly tales, of werewolves, of men turned by night into monstrous creatures. The memory became an obsession.

She had other work to do, of course. The Blair General Hospital knew how to get plenty from its nurses. But still she felt that at any moment one of those subdued, gurgling moans from 412 would turn into a screech of animal rage or fear. Yet no one else seemed to guess. There was the same simpering, the same babbling among the other nurses. Then the thing came, all the more frightful because she had been half expecting it, like a blow falling on a tensed body. If the door of the sick room was closed, the scream knifed through it with a daggerpoint. Nurses are as tough-minded as any people in the world, but the five in the floor-office turned white and stared at one another with a dreadful surmise. It was not one scream but a series of them. She did not need to hunt for the source of the outcry. She went straight to 412 and found the door ajar and the yell coming out of it. She shut the door hastily behind her as she went in. The mouth of Thornton was open, awry, and he screamed on every outgoing breath. Kildare was giving an injection. As he pulled the hypodermic away, he gave the nurse a quick look over his shoulder that made her flesh creep. She had never known what it meant to be afraid of a man but she was afraid now.

There was a firm rap at the door.

'Keep them out!' commanded Kildare.

Mary Lamont went to the door and found Miss Simmons, the head nurse of the floor.

'I must go in there,' said Miss Simmons, firmly.

'The doctor wants to be left alone, Miss Simmons,' she said.

'Wants to be left alone? What doctor, please?'

'Dr. Kildare.'

'The interne?'

'Yes, Miss Simmons.'

'Has he authority from Dr. Lane to take charge of this patient?'

'Yes, Miss Simmons.'

'Ah, he has?'

'Yes, Miss Simmons.'

'Very well,' said the head nurse, but she turned slowly away, her eyes lingering on the guilty face of Mary Lamont.

The screaming had died away, but still the girl wanted nothing so much as to be away from that room. She had to fight hard to make herself turn and look at the bed. The one lamp threw the shadow of Kildare in caricature, like a stain of soot, across the white of the bedspread and over the hands of Thornton, but the face of the patient was visible. It was fallen in complete relaxation.

'Take his temperature,' said Kildare.

He put a tongue depressor between the teeth of Thornton as though he feared the thermometer might be bitten in two. The nurse slipped the thermometer under the tongue.

'Hold his lips together,' said Kildare, and shone his light again into one of Thornton's eyes.

She pressed the lips shut. Foam kept breaking out in small bubbles. The mouth was cold; the lips were bluish. It was like handling wet clay.

She waited two minutes and drew out the thermometer.

'I'll get another thermometer,' she said. 'This one is no good.'

'The thermometer is all right,' he answered. 'What does it say?'

'It can't be right—and the man still alive,' she said. 'It only says eighty-five, Doctor!'

That was all he was to her, now. He wasn't Kildare. He was a sort of predatory beast drawing the life out of this helpless man.

'Eighty-five?' repeated Kildare.

'Yes, eighty-five. He isn't really living. He's dead—he's dying now!'

'Maybe,' said Kildare, and put that light to the inhuman eye of Thornton once more.

She found herself backing up toward the door. He took the stethoscope from his ears and said: 'Have you seen the special?'

'Not for hours,' she answered.

'That's queer,' said Kildare.

He talked as though he were drunk, with loose lips and a thick tongue. She got farther back, toward the door.

'Are you afraid?' asked Kildare.

She said nothing.

'Come here,' said Kildare.

She got her feet somehow across the floor to him.

'I'm ashamed of you,' he said, looking up at her. 'Go on about your work. I don't want you here.'

He looked back to Thornton and wiped the foam from the mouth of the sick man.

'I'm not afraid any more,' said Mary Lamont. 'I'll do anything you want, Doctor.'

'What did the Simmons have to say to you?'

'She wanted to know if you had authority from Dr. Lane to handle this case. Of course I told her you did.'

'Go back to her and say you lied. I haven't any authority.'

She felt a dreadful certainty that she was closed into the room with two madmen, not one. The thing to do is to humor the mad.

'I won't go to her. I won't tell her,' she said.

'Take his temperature again,' he commanded.

She went about the work once more.

Kildare took the utterly loose arm of Thornton and bent it up and down several times. Mary Lamont drew the thermometer from the clammy mouth and shuddered as she read it.

'Still eighty-five, Doctor,' she said.

'Eighty-five,' murmured Kildare. 'My God, eighty-five.'

It was plain that he had spoken to himself, not to her and the fear that had been growing in her sprang out like an electric current, tingling in her forehead and down through the tips of her fingers.

Then, not like a living creature but as though to make a mockery of sentient motion, the arm of Thornton which Kildare had flexed began to lift and fall in the same

99

gesture, and presently he tried to sit up, still with his eyes closed; and again it was like movement in the dead. Thornton swayed his head; he was like a man trying to catch his balance on a running horse.

Kildare pressed him back into the bed.

A new knock came at the door.

'Keep them out,' said the emotionless voice of Kildare.

But when the girl opened the door she saw Dr. Carew himself in the hall.

'You are Nurse Lamont, aren't you?' he asked. And he went on: 'I understand Kildare is in here?'

'Yes, sir. He wished to work without interruption, sir.'

'Does he?' said Carew, and walked straight in, past her, almost as though he would have walked over her.

He was not a big man but anger enlarged him.

'Kildare,' he said, 'were you authorized to take care of this case tonight?' Then he took full note of Thornton's face and exclaimed: 'By God, I think you've killed that man! Kildare!'

Kildare lifted his head a little but failed to turn it.

'This is Dr. Carew speaking,' said the head of the hospital.

'Very well,' said Kildare, never moving his eyes from the face of Thornton.

'Very well? But it's distinctly not very well!' said Carew, his voice kept down, his rage only a tremor of tension, in the dying presence of Thornton. 'What authority have you to take charge of this case, I repeat?'

'None,' said Kildare. 'This is entirely on my own.'

Carew rose to his tiptoes. He settled back on his heels more slowly.

'Leave this room and get back to your own place in the hospital,' he said. 'I had something to tell the board about you tomorrow, now I shall have enough more. Leave this patient instantly!'

'Who'll take him in charge if I go?' asked Kildare. 'Does anybody else want the responsibility, now?' He turned at last and gave to Carew a ghastly smile.

'What have you done to him, man?' demanded Carew.

A groan from Thornton seemed to give the answer. Carew, hesitating an instant, turned and walked rapidly from the room. He slammed the door heavily after him, regardless of dead or dying patients.

Mary Lamont went out after him. She could not stand it a moment longer in the room. Daylight was coming. She leaned at an open window and told herself that the coming day gave more life and more hope to the very air she was breathing. After a few minutes she was able to go back.

The daylight made things worse instead of better. It showed the senseless face of Thornton and the white torment in that of Kildare far better than the lamps had done.

'Tell me how to help,' she pleaded.

'Nobody can help me,' he said. 'Not now. Nobody in the hospital. But keep looking back in on me when you can, will you?'

She glanced at his preparations. There was a flat dish, a rubber tube, a hypodermic, and a reddish solution in a stoppered flask. She could make no sense out of them, and she went away again. There were things for her to do. She got through them mechanically and then hurried back, carrying a tray of coffee and thin sandwiches.

Kildare, bunch-backed like an old man, leaned over the bed at watch, as he had been all those hours. There seemed little left of him. It was fantastically as though he were giving up part of his own life in order to take that of Thornton. There was something between Thornton's teeth on which he bit with locked jaws. His whole body seemed as stiff as stone, with the fists clenched, the hands turning slowly in, the arms extending themselves. In that spastic rigidity she recognized the last stage of life. Men died, a little after they reached that point. Kildare seemed to be dying with his patient. When she offered him the coffee he was unaware of it, though the steam rose into his face.

'Take this,' she ordered.

He discovered the coffee with vague surprise and took the cup in his hand. Once more he forgot everything except the dying man on the bed.

'Drink it,' she commanded.

He discovered the coffee again, tasted it, drank it. She pulled the empty cup from his fingers. She stepped back and looked at him. A fist fight hardly could have battered and discolored his eyes more. 'Where is he—now?' she asked.

The weary eyes did not shift for an instant from Thornton, as though the grip they kept upon him were what tied him to life.

'He's back at the beginning of things,' said Kildare. 'He's gone through all the stages of evolution in reverse. His brain has been scaled away in layers, and now he's back in the stage of the reptile. Nothing in his brain is alive except the medulla, the very base of it; and the only thing that brain can tell his muscles to do is to twist and writhe, with movements like those of a snake.'

He spoke slowly, a phrase at a time, pauses between. As he finished speaking, he forgot her.

'Will he—will he live?' she managed to ask.

'Get some blood out of an artery for me,' said Kildare.

She prepared a syringe, and tried for the

big artery at the inside of the elbow. She knew the hypodermic needle found that artery, but the blood that came out was thick, viscous, dead, like the blood from a vein.

'Look!' she said, whispering. 'It's from an artery, but there's no life in it. It's the same as blood from a vein...'

'Very well. Stop screaming at me!'

The loud-speaker in his own brain had turned her voice to thunder, no doubt.

'Yes, Doctor,' she said. 'What else can I do?' He did not hear.

She crouched by his chair and looked up in his face. It was as though he had been away from her for years, he was so twisted and hardened by the endurance of those long hours. Yet her heart opened suddenly to him.

She said: 'Jimmy, tell me how to share it with you, and help!'

He was silent.

She repeated: 'Are you sure what will happen to him?'

'No,' said Kildare. 'All I know is that I have to nearly kill his brain before I can hope that he'll wake up into a few minutes of sanity.'

'But suppose he doesn't wake up?'

'Then I've murdered him,' said Kildare.

She got a good grip on the foot of the bed and steadied herself.

'What time is it?' he asked, never dropping his eyes from the face of Thornton.

'It's after seven,' she said.

'Thank God!' he said. 'Leave me alone with him ... and then come back.'

She went out. There was still no sign of Carew returning. Before he came back, no doubt he would have the career of Kildare already nailed on a cross. A rumor had gone through the hospital. There were plenty of people in the corridor, now, from nurses and attendants to staff physicians.

Molly Byrd, grim as a Roman soldier, bore down on the girl and cornered her.

'What's going on in 412?' she asked. 'Carew's half mad!'

'I don't know,' said Mary Lamont.

'Don't be a fool!' said the Byrd. 'Don't be a nitwit—*you!* What's the matter with you, Lamont? Have you seen a ghost? Come here and let me get some hot coffee into you!'

She dragged Mary Lamont into the floor office and poured some steaming coffee. The girl sat shuddering in a chair with her hands pressed to her face.

'Talk to me now,' commanded the Byrd, when Mary had swallowed some coffee.

'I can't,' said the girl. 'I can't say anything ... it's too horrible ... I mean...'

'If I can't get anything out of you, I'll use my own eyes and ears,' said the head nurse.

'Don't go into that room!' cried Mary.

Something about her voice was enough to stop Molly Byrd at the door.

'Why not?' she demanded.

'I don't know—except that it will haunt you every day of your life.'

Even the Byrd was impressed. Mary went past her into the hall.

'I've *got* to get back there,' said Mary.

When she was inside the room, she saw that the whole thing had changed. It was much more frightful to a casual eye but not to the eye of a nurse. Thornton foamed at the mouth and slobbered, turning his head from side to side with sudden movements. But life was coming back. The attitude of Kildare was altered, also. He was no longer like a murderer but what she knew of old—all eager brain and tenacious will. The period of mute waiting had ended.

He wiped the foam from the mouth of Thornton. He kept saying: 'Thornton, how are you? How is it now, Thornton?'

Kildare turned and nodded his head toward the door. The girl, as she went out, kept remembering that last look, for there was an uncanny brightness of triumph in it.

'Noon, Friday ... where is it you have to be? What is it you have to do, Thornton ... Noon, Friday—Thornton, what is it you have to do at noon, Friday?'

The head of Thornton at last stopped rolling. Light entered the blank mist of his

106

open eyes.

'I meet Marian—in the lobby of the Clerfayt Hotel—at noon, Friday,' he said. He roused suddenly and completely, crying out: 'Will you get me there?'

He caught at the hands of Kildare and repeated in an agony: 'Will you get me there?'

CHAPTER SIXTEEN

Ten or fifteen minutes later a sort of quiet maelstrom in the form of Dr. Carew had picked up Mary Lamont. He had Gregory Lane with him. He was saying to Lane: 'I simply want a direct understanding on one point which already has been put to you: Did you or did you not order definite work to be done on Thornton tonight, or did you give indefinite authority to any other doctor in the hospital to interfere with that patient?'

'No,' said Lane, 'I did not.'

He looked curiously at Carew and then at Mary.

Carew had turned on her, as they walked briskly down the corridor, saying: 'Now, Nurse Lamont, I want from you a detailed report on what has been going on in Room 412 last night and this morning.'

'Mr. Thornton seemed very ill,' she said.

'Dr. Kildare was with him...'

'Doing what?'

'I can't tell, Doctor. I was not given the full details of the treatment...'

'It was written on the chart, was it not?'

'I believe not, sir.'

Carew came to an abrupt halt. He was purple with his emotion.

'An uncharted treatment—given without permission—by an *interne!* ... It's on Gillespie's head, eventually! Eventually on his head...'

He started forward again, walking with violent speed.

He exclaimed: 'To encourage the ignorant bullheadedness of a boy—a mere child! To place in his hands the authority of an experienced physician! God forgive them both, but the Blair Hospital never! ... You are well out of this, young Dr. Lane! It is very well for you that you performed your operation with the apparent authorization of Gillespie through his baby-faced assistant, otherwise we should...'

'I beg your pardon, Dr. Carew,' said Lane. 'I was my own single authority for that operation. Authorization, did you say? From Dr. Gillespie through Kildare? There was not a word from either of them!'

Carew stopped again and passed a handkerchief across his forehead. 'I hope I'm not going quite mad,' he said. 'Do you mean to say that when correction was about to fall on you—like a sword, in fact—another man dared to stand between you and—Dr. Lane, how in God's name does this make the slightest sense?'

'Did Kildare tell you that he had authorized the operation in the name of Dr. Gillespie?' demanded Lane.

'He did. In my office. In almost exactly those words.'

Lane shook his head slowly, bewildered.

'I can't understand it,' he said. 'God knows it was not from any friendship. We're strangers, practically...'

'Let's get on to Kildare. In the old days,' said Carew, as he hurried forward again, 'all roads led to Rome, and when there is trouble in the Blair Hospital, apparently all roads lead to young Dr. Kildare—a state of affairs which presently may be remedied—very presently!'

They came to Room 412. There were twenty people curiously looking on at various distances in the corridor.

'Shall I go in first, Dr. Carew?' asked Mary Lamont.

'We'll have no forerunners,' said Carew. 'Let him take the full brunt, as he deserves to take it! *You* shall enter first, Dr. Lane!'

That was the order of entrance, Lane first, with Carew behind him, and Mary Lamont closing the door hastily behind them to shut out as much of the expected scene as possible from the eyes and the ears of the people in the hall.

But Kildare was not there. They had before them only Henry Thornton with an extra pillow cushioning his head. The dimness and the wandering was utterly gone from his eye.

'Good morning,' he said. 'I hope you're bringing those jelly sandwiches that Dr. Kildare promised me? And the milk?'

The rage of Dr. Carew, quite ready to be poured forth even in the presence of an insane patient, was checked at its source by this revelation. He went slowly toward the bed, holding out his hand a little, in an attitude humorously like that of a man approaching a flighty horse.

'My dear Mr. Thornton,' he said, 'do you feel quite well?'

'Extraordinarily well,' said Thornton, too full of smiles to attempt to control them. 'I seem to have been quite ill—or else I've been having very bad dreams.'

'Chiefly dreams, Mr. Thornton—chiefly dreams, my dear fellow,' said Carew.

He seemed to have forgotten everything else in a good doctor's delight in an unexpected cure. 'Chiefly dreams,' repeated Carew, 'and rather a bad knock in the head.'

'Silly of me to be bowled over like that, wasn't it?' said Thornton, almost laughing.

'But do you mind me bringing up the subject of those jelly sandwiches, if you please? I'm half starved.'

'You shall have a mountain of them,' said Carew. 'You shall have a whole mountain of them ... And did Dr. Kildare leave you very long ago?'

'Hardly five minutes, I believe,' said Thornton, still with that cheerful smile.

Here a special nurse came in with a whole tray of sandwiches and a bottle of milk with melted frost running down its sides.

'Ah, here it comes!' said Thornton, reaching out a welcoming hand. 'This is a very pleasant sight, nurse!'

The special, seeing the change in him, almost dropped the tray. She threw a wild glance toward Carew, who said instantly: 'We seem to be quite out of the woods, this morning. Quite out of the woods, indeed!'

The head of the hospital withdrew from the room with Lane and Mary Lamont. He stood bewildered, but still smiling, in the corridor.

'I saw him yesterday,' said Carew, 'and the poor fellow's condition wrung my heart! To see a change like this—it's a reward that makes a life of work seem a small thing, doesn't it, Lane?'

'It does, sir,' said Gregory Lane.

They smiled on one another.

'It's an act of God!' said Carew. 'Nothing

111

else could have made the change in him so quickly. It's an act of God!'

'Or of Dr. Kildare?' suggested Mary Lamont softly.

'Ha? Kildare?' echoed Carew. 'Extraordinary, damned, difficult young scoundrel ... Nurse, what *did* he do to Thornton last night?'

'I don't know,' she said, brokenly. 'But it seemed to be his own life that he was taking in his hands!'

'I don't blame you,' said Carew, patting her shoulder. 'I don't blame tears. It's the rarest thing in the world when a man ventures his reputation, his career, his whole future, his whole honor, and in spite of the confounded rule-makers like Walter Carew, dares to be right ... a damned touching thing!'

He went off down the corridor in a happy dream, still shaking his head.

'You're knocked to pieces; you've been through a pretty thick slice of hell, I think,' said Gregory Lane. 'Let me take you somewhere so that people won't stare at you, dear.'

'I'm all right,' she said. But she was trembling as she added: 'He's done it before, and he's only saved himself by being right ... but someday he'll put his neck in the noose for other people, and it won't turn out this way. Some day it'll go wrong; and then all his work, and all his life, will be ruined! Don't you see, Gregory?'

'It's Kildare you mean,' said Lane, looking intently at her.

'He's always committing himself to the lost causes,' she said. 'And someday the ship will sink under him, and take him down with it!'

'I've got to find him,' said Lane.

'I'll go along,' she agreed.

CHAPTER SEVENTEEN

But Mary Lamont and Dr. Lane found no trace of Kildare in the hospital. Noon came and there was no Kildare in Gillespie's office. Stephen Kildare came in at that time to say he had been a trifle worried about his son when he last saw him that morning.

'*When* did you see him?' asked Gillespie.

'About eight-thirty this morning,' said old Kildare. 'Isn't he back at the hospital?'

'There's no sign of him,' said Gillespie. 'What was he talking about when you saw him?'

'He asked for fifty dollars.'

'For what?'

'I don't know.'

'You mean, you didn't give it to him?'

'Oh, yes. I happened to have that much, so

of course I gave it to him.'

'Ha!' growled Gillespie. 'You had the money so *of course* you gave it to him ... And then what?'

'He took a hot bath, a pony of brandy, a cup of coffee, and left at once.'

'Without saying a word of where he was going?'

'No, Doctor.'

At seven that night there still was no Kildare. Gillespie telephoned to Carew.

'Will you come down to see me, or shall I come up to see you?' he asked.

'Is it important?'

'It's as important as the devil, to me.'

'I'll come down,' said Carew.

When he reached the office of Gillespie, the diagnostician was in a strange smiling humor but it was one that was familiar to Carew and he looked instantly askance at the great man.

'I hear that Henry Thornton is much better, Walter,' he said, genially.

'Much, much better,' said Carew.

'Then Lane's to be congratulated for his fine work, eh?'

'Not altogether Lane. Your man Kildare seems to have turned the trick last night.'

'Not the young interne! Not the stupid young fool you were going to run out of the hospital, Walter!'

Carew said nothing. He seemed to see

114

what was coming.

'As a matter of fact,' said Gillespie, 'I'm really astonished to hear what you have to say. The truth is that I thought you'd lived up to your word—I thought that you *had* run Kildare out of the hospital!'

'Nonsense, Leonard,' said the head of the hospital. 'You know perfectly well that I never would have taken final action without first warning you.'

'Then why isn't he here?' roared Gillespie.

'Here? In this office?'

'Yes, or in the entire hospital. There's no sign of him! What did you do with him, Carew?'

'Nothing, Leonard. Not a thing. I did *not* dismiss him.'

'What did you last say to him?'

'I don't remember the exact words.'

'Damn the exact words. What was the *intent?* Did you leave him feeling that he was on a good basis with you and the hospital?'

'I'm afraid not. Leonard, I want you to consider the case of a mere interne who pretends to have used your name to authorize a dangerous operation; and who then without permission from the doctor in charge invades the room of a patient and seems on the verge of killing him with a treatment which is not even written down on the chart!'

'Do you think that every man in the world

is a fool or a criminal unless he stands your height, has your weight, and fits your shoes? Are we going to have nothing in the world but Prussian disciplinarians like Walter Carew? Are you going to deny to young physicians the chance to use the brain and imagination that God gave them, so that you can lead them around by apron strings? Is that what you want?' thundered Gillespie.

'Every word you say is unfair,' complained Carew.

'You've frightened Kildare out of this hospital, out of medicine, out of his chance to serve the world,' declared Gillespie. 'Go back and sit down with the thought. It will be a warm comfort for you. And remember all the time that you've remained inside your rights. By God, Carew, I call what you've done, intellectual murder!'

Carew did not stay to argue; he walked soundlessly from the office, a small and shrinking figure.

At fifteen minutes before noon, on this Friday, a telephone call was put through to Gregory Lane. The voice of Kildare came none too clearly to him.

'Hai, Jimmy!' called Lane. 'Where are you, fellow? There's been a regular manhunt and hell to pay, trying to find you. Where are you?'

'Authorize them to connect me with Thornton,' said Kildare.

'The trouble is that Thornton is none too well,' said Lane. 'He was bright and fine for a number of hours after you treated him, but then...'

'This is long distance and I haven't much money. I don't care what his condition is. Put me through to him!'

They put Kildare through to Thornton. Lane, sweating with anxiety, hovered at the door of the room. Mary Lamont was inside it, listening. She held to the ear of Thornton the telephone receiver which his hands did not seem able to hold. Thin as a spider thread she heard the voice of Kildare coming over, saying: 'Thornton, I'm here in Clerfayt and she's with me. Marian is with me and everything is all right.'

'Marian? Where is she?' cried Thornton. His hand suddenly grasped the receiver and he sat up in the bed.

'She's here, in Clerfayt, but we're leaving right away. She's coming back to you, Thornton. We're coming back as fast as an airplane can take us. And she's going to stay with you forever. Do you hear me? Can you understand me?' Jimmy asked.

'I hear you! I hear you!' exclaimed Thornton.

'Good-by, then—and be patient—she's a happy girl!' said the far away voice of Kildare, and his receiver clicked.

Thornton still held the instrument to his

ear as though he were draining further happiness from it.

'He's made it for me,' said Thornton, whispering, half to himself and half to Mary Lamont. 'He's there with her, in time. And she'll be with me all the days of my life!'

CHAPTER EIGHTEEN

But Kildare was not with Marian Thornton in the town of Clerfayt. It doesn't take a crow long to fly from Denver to Clerfayt, but the automobile road is a winding nightmare that loops among the mountains like a tangled lariat and the bus in which Kildare was a passenger had broken down while it was still ten miles from the destination.

'I've got an hour to reach Clerfayt,' he said to the saloonkeeper, 'and I've got a dollar and fifteen cents to rent a horse. I know it's not enough.'

'Sure it ain't,' said the saloonkeeper. 'Besides, I ain't got a horse. But there's a mule out there that's better than any horse in the mountains, and I might loan him to you, stranger.'

That was how Kildare happened to ride a long-legged gray mule down the last ragged slope and into the town of Clerfayt. He was already a half hour late when he jumped down in front of the Clerfayt Hotel and hurried into the lobby. There were only three people in it, the clerk in shirt-sleeves behind the desk, a big, brown-faced man and a pretty woman who sat beside him. They got up and started for the door as Kildare came in.

'You're Marian Thornton?' said Kildare.

She stopped and looked quickly up at the big fellow.

'You see, Jerry?' she said.

'Why didn't he come himself?' asked Jerry. 'Why did he have to send a messenger?'

'Because he's in a hospital,' said Kildare. 'I got here by plane and bus and mule-back; and I see that I'm barely in time ... Will you talk to me alone for a few moments?'

'I'll wait outside,' said Jerry.

Kildare sat in a corner with the girl. She was less pretty at close range than from a distance, but there was a wealth of cheerful color in her face. She asked no questions at all, but waited for information. Kildare liked that, and the way she sat straight up.

He said: 'I'm a doctor. My name is Kildare. Thornton is an accident case who was brought into the emergency room. We had to operate for fracture. He wouldn't accept the operation. He said he had a date line to meet. Friday—noon. He wanted to walk out. But he fainted before he could leave.'

She put up a hand to her face. He pitied the pain in it.

'We operated anyway. A very brilliant surgeon—Gregory Lane—and the operation was a success, but when Thornton found out that he was under restraint, and couldn't get out here to meet that date line—it was too much for his nerves.'

He paused there.

'You mean—his mind?' she asked.

'Yes,' said Kildare.

She closed her eyes. He said nothing.

'He *did* want me,' she said, at last.

'For five years,' said Kildare.

'If I go to him, do you think I can be the least help?' she asked.

'I think you can,' said Kildare.

'But you're not sure?'

'No.'

She turned and looked out the window. A pine tree grew across the road from the hotel, but the immense bulk of it almost filled the window. Every bough was big enough to make a respectable tree in Connecticut.

After a time she said: 'I'll get my things together. Do you know the quickest way to reach him?'

'Wait a minute,' said Kildare. 'Do you know what may lie ahead of you?'

'No. But I can guess,' she answered.

'Have you ever seen anything of the sort?'

'Yes, I've seen it. But it's better to fill your life with pain than with emptiness.'

'You've got more than emptiness. That big Jerry, yonder, wants to marry you.'

She looked at Kildare, a little surprised. There was a great stillness about her and a suggestion of strength as ample as a Western horizon.

'I suppose,' said Kildare, 'that that was the reason for the date line. You'd give Thornton his chance to reach for you, if he cared to. If not, there'd be Jerry.'

'He seemed to think that I'd be worth something to him. So I didn't have a right to deny him, you see, because I'm worth nothing to myself. But then I wondered if Henry might remember me and want me, after all. So I wrote. I hoped, in a vague sort of way, that he might forgive me.'

'He thinks that he's the one who needs forgiveness.'

'Because he was a bit of a sinner?'

She closed her eyes suddenly and bit her lip.

'Steady,' said Kildare.

'I won't cry,' she said. 'But when I think of the five years I threw away...'

'I know,' said Kildare.

'Is there any ghost of a chance that he might be himself again—just dimly—just now and then?' she asked.

121

Kildare took her hand.

'I've been a swine,' he said, 'but I wanted to find out what you are. Now I know. The fact is that there are nineteen chances out of twenty that he'll be perfect, after a little treatment and a good deal of you.'

She held hard to his hand.

'Whether you want me to or not,' she said, 'I'm going to believe every word.'

CHAPTER NINETEEN

It was late on Saturday when Nurse Parker broke sharply in on Dr. Gillespie.

He said angrily: 'What are you at me about now, Parker? I'm seeing no patients this morning.'

'Dr. Kildare has just come back—he's here—he's right in the hospital!' exclaimed Nurse Parker.

'What are you talking about?' said Gillespie. 'Kildare? Who said he was back?'

'I saw him! I saw him with my own eyes!'

'You did?' Gillespie pushed himself up in his chair. 'What excuse does the young fool give for playing hooky? What does he—I'm going to give him the dressing down of his life! Discipline? Carew? Before I'm through with him, I'll make him think he never heard of discipline before! Next patient!'

Gregory Lane, coming out of Room 412, met Kildare coming down the corridor with a handsome, open-faced girl of twenty-six or seven, a sun-browned young woman who carried her head high and looked the world straight in the eye.

Kildare said: 'This is the doctor I told you about ... This is Mrs. Thornton, Dr. Lane.'

She gave Lane's hand a strong, lingering pressure. She said, gravely: 'Dr. Kildare has told me what you did. I won't try to thank you, Doctor. I'll *never* try! ... But—may I see Henry now?'

'You understand his condition?' asked Lane, anxiously.

'She knows,' said Kildare, 'but he's much better than he was, isn't he?'

Lane stared at him. 'Much, much better,' he said.

There was a quick whispering of skirts down the hall. Mary Lamont was hurrying toward them.

'If you'll be very quiet, Mrs. Thornton,' said Lane, 'I'll take you in to him.'

'May I make a suggestion?' asked Kildare. 'May she go in to him alone?'

Lane, studying him, suddenly smiled. 'I've an idea that you know this case better than I do,' he said. 'If *you* think it's right—certainly, Mrs. Thornton! You may go in alone.'

She touched the arm of Kildare. 'Thank

you, Jimmy,' she said, and went softly into the room.

The two doctors stood with Mary Lamont at the door, which was slightly ajar.

'Jimmy—Jimmy—Jimmy!' whispered the girl and held out her hand as though she wanted to touch him and make sure he was there.

Lane looked at her curiously, steadily.

The voice of the sick man in Room 412 was saying: 'Closed in the wrong day—and I've got to get out—out of the wrong day—'

It was like someone talking in a dream.

They heard the voice of Marian Thornton, not the words but the music of it; and then Thornton himself speaking more loudly her name in a clear voice with all the sleepy, obscure drawl gone from it.

Kildare soundlessly shut the door.

'I'm guessing at it,' said Lane. 'It was insulin! You sneaked up here and used insulin shock! How did you dare to do it, man? How did you dare to bring him that close to dying?'

'But he's going to be cured,' said Kildare. 'And half the treatment is in there with him now. He waited five years for her but she's worth all the pain.'

Lane looked at Mary Lamont gravely, but still strangely without pain. 'I think there ought to be a little celebration for this. Here are the tickets to that show we were taking in tonight, Mary. You'll enjoy it more with Kildare.'

'I can't do that,' said Kildare.

Mary Lamont, watching Lane, said nothing at all, and out of her silence a quiet grew that embraced them all.

'I saw you, just now, when you met Kildare,' said Lane. 'You'd never have an eye like that for me in a thousand years. And I'm the sort of a fool that has to be head man, not second best ... You two will find a way to be happy. Let me know when I can congratulate you.'

He turned his back and then walked off.

'Call him back!' urged Kildare.

She shook her head.

'You're being a fool!' he said. 'You'll never find better as long as you live!'

'I know,' she agreed. 'You and I are both fools. Maybe that's why we need one another.'

★　　　★　　　★

In the office of Gillespie, Kildare found his father in excited conversation with the great man.

'I thought she was going to die,' said Stephen Kildare. 'It was almost a complete collapse. What had caused it? I couldn't guess. There was nothing at all dangerous. Only a diet low in salt. She begged to have some of her infernal brew of herbs. I had some stewed up to quiet her. I even tasted the stuff ... and suddenly I understood what it was that had been helping her in that witches' brew. The herbs had been packed in thick layers of salt to preserve them. It was a highly saline solution that she was drinking—and the salt...'

'Was what she needed!' exclaimed Gillespie.

'Of course, it was. You and I have missed it completely. All our years of experience and our laboratories hadn't helped her as much as her homemade tea, because what troubled her is...'

'Addison's Disease!' the two old men cried in one voice.

'A pair of old fools,' said Gillespie. 'And yet there was no pigmentation of the exposed areas of the skin...'

'A borderline case, in fact.'

'Now we can make her live twenty years, I hope.'

'I hope so—I think so. Jimmy, that two dollars you're holding—give it to charity. We've just proved that instinct and a bit of luck sometimes can beat all the doctors there are.'

'Young Dr. Kildare,' said Gillespie, 'I hear that you've brought home the bacon again. Otherwise I'd have given you the devil ... What did you use on him? Insulin?'

'Insulin—and a sort of prayer,' said Kildare. 'And luckily there wasn't even a special in the room all night to bother me.'

'Oh, the special nurse disappeared, did she?'

'Yes, sir.'

'She couldn't have been called away, could she?' asked Gillespie.

'Ah, did you do that?' demanded Kildare.

'I can tell a crime when it first begins to swim into the eye of the criminal, like a fish up to the surface of a pond. I knew you'd need to be alone.'

*　　*　　*

'It's as though a tidal wave had gone over me, and now I'm back in the air, breathing and blinking again,' said Kildare to Mary Lamont that night. 'And are you *sure* that you're right, being here with me?'

'Five years—' said the girl. 'Poor Henry Thornton waited five years—so why should I complain if I have to wait a while for Jimmy Kildare? I've turned into an old-fashioned girl.'

'You won't feel that way about it tomorrow. There doesn't seem to be the least glimmer of a prospect ahead of us.'

'There is, though,' said the girl. 'There's hope, you know.'

'Yes,' said Kildare. 'There's a bit of that,

of course.'

'And there's the sense of coming back to you, and it's like coming home.'

'That's it. And that's something,' said Kildare. 'We don't have to add up what we have and see what it amounts to.'

'Of course, we don't, and we always have everything that lies between good morning and good night.'

Max Brand™ is the best-known pen name of Frederick Faust, creator of Dr. Kildare™, Destry, and many other fictional characters popular with readers and viewers worldwide. Faust wrote for a variety of audiences in many genres. His enormous output, totaling approximately thirty million words or the equivalent of 530 ordinary books, covered nearly every field: crime, fantasy, historical romance, espionage, Westerns, science fiction, adventure, animal stories, love, war, and fashionable society, big business and big medicine. Eighty motion pictures have been based on his work along with many radio and television programs. For good measure he also published four volumes of poetry. Perhaps no other author has reached more people in more different ways.

Born in Seattle in 1892, orphaned early, Faust grew up in the rural San Joaquin Valley of California. At Berkeley he became a student rebel and one-man literary movement, contributing prodigiously to all campus publications. Denied a degree because of unconventional conduct, he embarked on a series of adventures culminating in New York City where, after a period of near starvation, he received simultaneous recognition as a serious poet and successful popular-prose writer. Later, he traveled widely, making his home in New York, then in Florence, and finally in Los Angeles.

Once the United States entered the Second World War, Faust abandoned his lucrative writing career and his work as a screenwriter to serve as a war correspondent with the infantry in Italy, despite his fifty-one years and a bad heart. He was killed during a night attack on a hilltop village held by the German army. New books based on magazine serials or unpublished manuscripts continue to appear. Alive and dead he has averaged a new one every four months for seventy-five years. In the U.S. alone nine publishers issue his work, plus many more in foreign countries. Yet, only recently have the full dimensions of this extraordinarily versatile and prolific writer come to be recognized and his stature as a protean literary figure in the 20th Century acknowledged. His popularity continues to grow throughout the world.